AF568077

ALEPH *olio*

WAYS OF DYING

One of the meanings of the word 'olio' is 'a miscellany'. The books in the Aleph Olio series contain a selection of the finest writing to be had on a variety of Indian themes–the great cities, aspects of culture and civilization, and other uniquely Indian phenomena. Filled with insights and haunting evocations of a country of unrivalled complexity, beauty, tragedy, and mystery, each Aleph Olio book presents India in ways that it has seldom been seen before.

Also in Aleph Olio

The Essence of Delhi
In a Violent Land
Love and Lust
Notes from the Hinterland
The Book of Indian Kings

WAYS OF DYING

Stories and Essays

ALEPH BOOK COMPANY
An independent publishing firm
promoted by ***Rupa Publications India***

First published in India in 2020
by Aleph Book Company
7/16 Ansari Road, Daryaganj
New Delhi 110 002

ISBN: 978-93-89836-14-1

1 3 5 7 9 10 8 6 4 2

For sale in the Indian subcontinent only.

Printed at Replika Press Pvt. Ltd, India

'Dying is just the same as going to sleep',
The piper whispered, 'close your eyes',
And blew some hints and whispers on his pipe:
The children closed their eyes

And gravely wandered in a private darkness,
Imagining death to be a way of looking.

—DOM MORAES, 'Figures in a Landscape'

A NOTE ON THE BOOK

In order to preserve the form and flavour of the pieces as they were originally published, the texts have not been standardized according to Aleph's house style. The epigraph is taken from 'Figures in a Landscape' by Dom Moraes.

CONTENTS

1. AMITAV GHOSH 1
The Ghosts of Mrs Gandhi

2. RUSKIN BOND 19
The Funeral

3. AMITAVA KUMAR 24
Pyre

4. MAHASWETA DEVI 36
Seed
Translated from the Bengali by Ipshita Chanda

5. ATUL GAWANDE 68
Being Mortal

6. MUNSHI PREMCHAND 75
The Shroud
Translated from the Urdu by Muhammad Umar Memon

7. KHUSHWANT SINGH 85
The Portrait of a Lady

8. GEORGE ORWELL 90
Shooting An Elephant

9. DAVID DAVIDAR 99
Death of a Patriarch

10. KOLAKALURI ENOCH 104
Hunger
Translated from the Telugu by C. L. L. Jayaprada

Acknowledgements 119

Notes on the Contributors 121

ONE

~

THE GHOSTS OF MRS GANDHI*

AMITAV GHOSH

Nowhere else in the world did the year 1984 fulfil its apocalyptic portents as it did in India. Separatist violence in the Punjab, the military attack on the great Sikh temple of Amritsar; the assassination of the Prime Minister, Mrs Indira Gandhi; riots in several cities; the gas disaster in Bhopal—the events followed relentlessly on each other. There were days in 1984 when it took courage to open the New Delhi papers in the morning.

Of the year's many catastrophes, the sectarian violence following Mrs Gandhi's death had the greatest effect on my life. Looking back, I see that the experiences of that period were profoundly important to my development as a writer; so much so that I have never attempted to write about them until now.

At that time, I was living in a part of New Delhi called Defence Colony—a neighbourhood of large, labyrinthine

*This essay is taken from *The Imam and the Indian: Prose Pieces* by Amitav Ghosh, published by Penguin Books, 2002.

houses, with little self-contained warrens of servants' rooms tucked away on rooftops and above garages. When I lived there, those rooms had come to house a floating population of the young and straitened journalists, copywriters, minor executives, and university people like myself. We battened upon this wealthy enclave like mites in a honeycomb, spreading from rooftop to rooftop, our ramshackle lives curtained from our landlords by chiffon-draped washing lines and thickets of TV aerials.

I was twenty-eight. The city I considered home was Calcutta, but New Delhi was where I had spent all my adult life except for a few years in England and Egypt. I had returned to India two years before, upon completing a doctorate at Oxford, and recently found a teaching job at Delhi University. But it was in the privacy of my baking rooftop hutch that my real life was lived. I was writing my first novel, in the classic fashion, perched in a garret.

On the morning of 31 October, the day of Mrs Gandhi's death, I caught a bus to Delhi University, as usual, at about half past nine. From where I lived, it took an hour and half: a long commute, but not an exceptional one for New Delhi. The assassination had occurred shortly before, just a few miles away, but I had no knowledge of this when I boarded the bus. Nor did I notice anything untoward at any point during the ninety-minute journey. But the news, traveling by word of mouth, raced my bus to the university.

When I walked into the grounds, I saw not the usual boisterous, Frisbee-throwing crowd of students but small groups of people standing intently around transistor radios. A young man detached himself from one of the huddles and approached me, his mouth twisted into the tight-lipped, knowing smile that seems always to accompany the gambit 'Have you heard...?'

The campus was humming, he said. No one knew for sure, but it was being said that Mrs Gandhi had been shot. The word was that she had been assassinated by two Sikh bodyguards, in revenge for her having sent troops to raid the Sikhs' Golden Temple of Amritsar earlier that year.

Just before stepping into the lecture room, I heard a report on All India Radio, the national network: Mrs Gandhi had been rushed to hospital after an attempted assassination.

Nothing stopped: the momentum of the daily routine carried things forward. I went into a classroom and began my lecture, but not many students had shown up and those who had were distracted and distant; there was a lot of fidgeting.

Halfway through the class, I looked out through the room's single, slit-like window. The sunlight lay bright on the lawn below and on the trees beyond. It was the time of year when Delhi was at its best, crisp and cool, its abundant greenery freshly watered by the recently retreated monsoons, its skies washed sparkling clean. By the time I turned back, I had forgotten what I was saying and had to reach for my notes.

My unsteadiness surprised me. I was not an uncritical admirer of Mrs Gandhi. Her brief period of semi-dictatorial rule in the mid-seventies was still alive in my memory. But the ghastliness of her sudden murder was a reminder of the very real qualities that had been taken for granted: her fortitude, her dignity, her physical courage, her endurance.

Yet it was just not grief I felt at the moment. Rather, it was a sense of something loose, of a mooring coming untied somewhere within.

~

The first reliable report of Mrs Gandhi's death was broadcast from Karachi, by Pakistan's official radio network, at around 1:30 p.m. On All India Radio, regular broadcasts had been replaced by music.

I left the university in the late afternoon with a friend, Hari Sen, who lived at the other end of the city. I needed to make a long-distance phone call, and he had offered to let me use his family telephone.

To get to Hari's house we had to change buses at Connaught Place, the elegant circular arcade that lies at the geographical heart of Delhi, linking the old city with the new. As the bus swung around the periphery of the arcade, I noticed that the shops, stalls, and eateries were beginning to shut down, even though it was still afternoon.

Our next bus was not quite full, which was unusual. Just as it was pulling out, a man ran out of the office and jumped on. He was middle-aged and dressed in shirt and trousers, evidently an employee in one of the government buildings. He was a Sikh, but I scarcely noticed this at the time.

He probably jumped on without giving the matter any thought, this being his regular, daily bus. But, as it happened, on this day no choice could have been more unfortunate, for the route of the bus went past the hospital where Indira Gandhi's body then lay. Certain loyalists in her party had begun inciting the crowds gathered there to seek revenge. The motorcade of Giani Zail Singh, the President of the Republic, a Sikh, had already been attacked by a mob.

None of this was known to us then, and we would never have suspected it: violence had never been directed at the Sikhs in Delhi.

As the bus made its way down New Delhi's broad, tree-lined avenues, official-looking cars, with outriders and escorts, overtook us, speeding towards the hospital. As we drew nearer, it became evident that a large number of people had gathered there. But this was no ordinary crowd: it seemed to consist of red-eyed young men in half-unbuttoned shirts. It was now that I noticed that my Sikh fellow-passenger was showing signs of anxiety, sometimes standing up to look out, sometimes glancing out the door. It was too late to get off the bus; thugs were everywhere. The bands of young men grew more and more menacing as we approached the hospital. There was a watchfulness about them; some were armed with steel rods and bicycle chains; others had fanned out across the busy road and were stopping cars and buses.

A stout woman in a sari sitting across the aisle from me was the first to understand what was going on. Rising to her feet, she gestured urgently at the Sikh, who was sitting hunched in his seat. She hissed at him in Hindi, telling him to get down and keep out of sight.

The man started in surprise and squeezed himself into the narrow foot space between the seats. Minutes later, our bus was intercepted by a group of young men dressed in bright, sharp synthetics. Several had bicycle chains wrapped around their wrists. They ran along beside the bus as it slowed to a halt. We heard them call out to the driver through the open door, asking if there were any Sikhs on the bus.

The driver shook his head. No, he said, there were no Sikhs on the bus.

A few rows ahead of me, the crouching, turbaned figure had gone completely still. Outside, some of the young men were jumping up to look through the windows, asking if there were any Sikhs on the bus. There was no anger in their voices; that was the most chilling thing of all.

No, someone said, and immediately other voices picked up the refrain. Soon all the passengers were shaking their heads and saying, no, no, let us go now, we have to get home.

Eventually, the thugs stepped back and waved us through. Nobody said a word as we sped away down Ring Road.

~

Hari Sen lived in one of New Delhi's recently developed residential colonies. It was called Safdarjang Enclave, and it was neatly and solidly middle-class, a neighbourhood of aspirations rather than opulence. Like most such New Delhi suburbs, the area had a mixed population: Sikhs were well represented.

A long street ran from end to end of the neighbourhood, like the spine of a comb, with parallel side streets running off it.

Hari lived at the end of one of those streets, in a fairly typical, big, one-storey bungalow. The house next door, however, was much grander and uncharacteristically daring in design. An angular structure, it was perched rakishly on stilts. Mr Bawa, the owner, was an elderly Sikh who had spent a long time abroad, working with various international organizations. For several years, he had resided in Southeast Asia; thus the stilts.

Hari lived with his family in a household so large and eccentric that it had come to be known among his friends as Macondo, after Gabriel Garcia Marquez's magical village. On this occasion, however, only his mother and teenage sister were at home. I decided to stay over.

It was a bright morning. When I stepped into the sunshine, I came upon a sight that I could never have imagined. In every direction, columns of smoke rose slowly into a limpid sky. Sikh houses and businesses were burning. The fires were so carefully targeted that they created an effect quite different from that of a general conflagration: it was like looking upward into the vault of some vast pillared hall.

The columns of smoke increased in number even as I stood outside watching. Some fires were burning a short distance away. I spoke to a passer-by and learned that several nearby Sikh houses had been looted and set on fire that morning. The mob had started at the far end of the colony and was working its way in our direction. Hindus and Muslims who had sheltered or defended Sikhs were also being attacked; their houses were being looted and burned.

It was still and quiet, eerily so. The usual sounds of rush-hour traffic were absent. But every so often we heard a speeding car or a motorcycle on the main street. Later, we discovered that these mysterious speeding vehicles were instrumental in directing the carnage that was taking place. Protected by certain politicians, 'organizers' were zooming around the city, assembling 'mobs' and transporting them to Sikh-owned houses and shops.

Apparently, the transportation was provided free. A civil-rights report published shortly afterward stated that this phase of violence 'began with the arrival of groups of armed people in tempo vans, scooters, motorcycles or trucks', and went on to say, 'With cans of petrol they went around the localities and systematically set fire to Sikh houses, shops and gurdwaras... The targets were primarily young Sikhs. They were dragged out, beaten up and then burned alive... In all the affected spots, a calculated attempt to terrorize the people was evident in the common tendency among the assailants to burn alive Sikhs on public roads.'

Fire was everywhere; it was the day's motif. Throughout the city, Sikh houses were being looted and then set on fire, often with their occupants still inside.

A survivor—a woman who lost her husband and three sons—offered the following account to Veena Das, a Delhi sociologist: 'Some people, the neighbours, one of my relatives, said it would be better if we hid in an abandoned house nearby. So my husband took our three sons and hid there. We locked the house from outside, but there was treachery in people's hearts. Someone must have told the crowd. They baited him to come out. Then they poured kerosene on that house. They burnt them alive. When I went there that night, the bodies of my sons were on the loft—huddled together.'

Over the next few days, some twenty-five hundred people died in Delhi alone. Thousands more died in other cities. The total death toll will never be known. The dead were overwhelmingly Sikh men. Entire neighbourhoods were gutted; tens of thousands of people were left homeless.

Like many other members of my generation, I grew up believing that mass slaughter of the kind that accompanied the Partition of India and Pakistan, in 1947, could never happen again. But that morning, in the city of Delhi, the violence had reached the same level of intensity.

∽

As Hari and I stood staring into the smoke-streaked sky, Mrs Sen, Hari's mother, was thinking of matters closer at hand. She was about fifty, a tall, graceful woman with a gentle, soft-spoken manner. In an understated way, she was also deeply religious, a devout Hindu. When she heard what was happening, she picked up the phone and called Mr and Mrs Bawa, the elderly Sikh couple next door, to let them know that they were welcome to come over. She met with an unexpected response: an awkward silence. Mrs Bawa thought she was joking, and wasn't sure whether to be amused or not.

Towards midday, Mrs Sen received a phone call: the mob was now in the immediate neighbourhood, advancing systematically from street to street. Hari decided that it was time to go over and have a talk with the Bawas. I went along.

Mr Bawa proved to be small, slight man. Although he was casually dressed, his turban was neatly tied and his beard was carefully combed and bound. He was puzzled by our visit. After a polite greeting, he asked what he could do for us. It fell to Hari to explain.

Mr Bawa had heard about Indira's assassination, of course, and he knew there had been some trouble. But he could not understand why these 'disturbances' should impinge on him or his wife. He had no more sympathy for Sikh terrorists than we did; his revulsion at the assassination was, if anything, even greater than ours. Not only was his commitment to India and the Indian State absolute but it was evident from his bearing that he belonged to the country's ruling elite.

How do you explain to someone who has spent a lifetime cocooned in privilege that a potentially terminal rent has appeared in the wrappings? We found ourselves faltering. Mr Bawa could not bring himself to believe that a mob might attack him.

By the time we left, it was Mr Bawa who was mouthing reassurances. He sent us off with jovial pats on our backs. He did not actually say 'Buck up', but his manner said it for him.

We were confident that the government would soon act to stop the violence. In India, there is a drill associated with civil disturbances: a curfew is declared; paramilitary units are deployed; in extreme cases, the Army marches to the stricken areas. No city in India is better equipped to perform this drill than New Delhi, with its huge security apparatus. We learned later that in some cities—Calcutta, for example, the state authorities did act promptly to prevent violence. But in New Delhi and in much of northern India, hour followed hour without a response. Every few minutes, we turned to the radio, hoping to hear that the Army had been ordered out. All we heard was mournful music and descriptions of Mrs Gandhi's lying in state; of coming and goings of dignitaries, foreign and national. The bulletins could have been messages from another planet.

As the afternoon progressed, we continued to hear reports of the mob's steady advance. Before long, it had reached the next alley; we could hear the voices; the smoke was everywhere. There was still no sign of the Army or the police.

Hari again called Mr Bawa, and now, with the flames visible from his windows, he was more receptive. He agreed to come over with his wife, just for a short while. But there was a problem: How? The two properties were separated by a shoulder-high wall, so it was impossible to walk from one house to the other except along the street.

I spotted a few thugs already at the end of the street. We could hear the occasional motorcycle, cruising slowly up and down. The Bawas could not risk stepping out into the street. They would be seen; the sun had dipped low in the sky, but it was still light. Mr Bawa balked at the thought of climbing over the wall; it seemed an insuperable obstacle at his age. But eventually Hari persuaded him to try.

We went to wait for them at the back of the Sens' house—in a spot that was well sheltered from the street. The mob seemed terrifyingly close, the Bawas reckless in their tardiness. A long time passed before the elderly couple finally appeared, hurrying towards us.

Mr Bawa had changed before leaving the house: he was neatly dressed, dapper even—in blazer and cravat. Mrs Bawa, a small, matronly woman, was dressed in a salwar and kameez. Their cook was with them, and it was with his assistance that they made it over the wall. The cook, who was Hindu, then returned to the house to stand guard.

Hari led the Bawas into the drawing room, where Mrs Sen was waiting, dressed in a chiffon sari. The room was large and well appointed, its walls hung with a rare and beautiful set of miniatures. With the curtains now drawn and the lamps lit, it was warm and welcoming. But all that lay between us and the mob in the street was a row of curtained French windows and a garden wall.

Mrs Sen greeted the elderly couple with folded hands as they came in. The three seated themselves in an intimate circle, and soon a silver tea tray appeared. Instantly, all constraint evaporated, and, to the tinkling of porcelain, the conversation turned to the staples of New Delhi drawing-room chatter.

I could not bring myself to sit down. I stood in the corridor, distracted, looking outside through the front entrance.

A couple of scouts on motorcycles had drawn up next door. They had dismounted and were inspecting the house, walking in among the concrete stilts, looking up into the house. Somehow, they got wind of the cook's presence and called him out.

The cook was very frightened. He was surrounded by thugs thrusting knives in his face and shouting questions. It was dark, and some were carrying kerosene torches. Wasn't it true, they shouted, that his employers were Sikhs. Where were they? Were they hiding inside? Who owned the house—Hindus or Sikhs?

Hari and I hid behind the wall between the two houses and listened to the interrogation. Our fates depended on this lone, frightened man. We had no idea what he would do: of how secure the Bawas were of his loyalties, or whether he might seek revenge for some past slight by revealing their whereabouts. If he did, both houses would burn.

Although stuttering in terror, the cook held his own. Yes, he said, yes, his employers were Sikhs, but they had left town; there was no one in the house. No, the house didn't belong to them; they were renting from a Hindu.

He succeeded in persuading most of the thugs, but a few eyed the surrounding houses suspiciously. Some appeared at the steel gates in front of us, rattling the bars.

We went up and positioned ourselves at the gates. I remember a strange sense of disconnection as I walked down the driveway, as though I was watching myself from somewhere very distant.

We took hold of the gates and shouted back: Get away! You have no business here. There's no one inside! The house is empty!

To my surprise, they began to drift away, one by one.

Just before this, I had stepped into the house to see how Mrs Sen and the Bawas were faring. The thugs were clearly audible in the lamp-lit drawing room; only a thin curtain shielded the interior from their view.

My memory of what I saw in the drawing room is uncannily vivid. Mrs Sen had a slight smile on her face as she poured a cup of tea for Mr Bawa. Beside her, Mrs Bawa, in a firm, unwavering voice, was comparing the domestic situations in New Delhi and Manila.

I was awed by their courage.

~

The next morning, I heard about a protest that was being organized at the large compound of a relief agency. When I arrived, a meeting was already underway, a gathering of seventy or eighty people.

The mood was sombre. Some of the people spoke of neighbourhoods that had been taken over by vengeful mobs. They described countless murders—mainly by setting the victims alight—as well as terrible destruction; the burning of Sikh temples, the looting of Sikh schools, the razing of Sikh homes and shops. The violence was worse than I had imagined. It was decided that the most effective initial tactic would be to march into one of the badly affected neighbourhoods and confront the rioters directly.

The group had grown to a hundred and fifty men and women, among them Swami Agnivesh, a Hindu ascetic; Ravi Chopra, a scientist and environmentalist; and a handful of opposition politicians, including Chandra Shekhar, who became Prime Minister for a brief period several years later.

The group was pitifully small by the standards of a city where crowds of several hundred thousand were routinely mustered for political rallies. Nevertheless, the members rose to their feet and began to march.

Years before, I had read a passage by V. S. Naipaul, which had stayed with me ever since. I have never been able to find it again, so this account is from memory. In his incomparable prose Naipaul describes a demonstration. He is in a hotel room, somewhere in Africa or South America; he looks down and sees people marching past. To his surprise, the sight fills him with an obscure longing, a kind of melancholy; he is aware of a wish to go out, to join, to merge his concerns with theirs. Yet he knows he never will; it is simply not in his nature to join crowds.

For many years, I read everything of Naipaul's I could lay my hands on; I couldn't have enough of him. I read him with the intimate, appalled attention that one reserves for one's most skilful interlocutors. It was he who first made it possible for me to think of myself as a writer, working in English.

I remembered the passage because I believed that I, too, was not a joiner, and in Naipaul's pitiless mirror I thought I had seen an aspect of myself rendered visible. Yet as this forlorn little group marched out of the shelter of the compound I did not hesitate for a moment: without a second thought, I joined.

The march headed first to Lajpat Nagar, a busy commercial

area a mile or so away. I knew the area. Though it was in New Delhi, its streets resembled the older parts of the city, where small cramped shops tended to spill out on to the footpaths.

We were shouting slogans as we marched: hoary Gandhian staples of peace and brotherhood from half a century before. Then, suddenly, we were confronted with a starkly familiar spectacle, an image of twentieth-century urban horror: burned-out cars, their ransacked interiors visible through smashed windows; debris and rubble everywhere. Blackened pots had been strewn along the street. A cinema had been gutted, and the charred faces of film stars stared out at us from half-burned posters.

As I think back to that march, my memory breaks down, details dissolve. I recently telephoned some friends who had been there. Their memories are similar to mine in only one respect: they, too, clung to one scene while successfully ridding their minds of the rest.

The scene my memory preserved is of a moment when it seemed inevitable that we would be attacked.

Rounding a corner, we found ourselves facing a crowd that was larger and more determined-looking than any other crowds that we had encountered. On each previous occasion, we had prevailed by marching at the thugs and engaging them directly, in dialogues that turned quickly into extended shouting matches. In every instance, we had succeeded in facing them down. But this particular mob was intent on confrontation. As its members advanced on us, brandishing knives and steel rods, we stopped. Our voices grew louder as they came towards us; a kind of rapture descended on us, exhilaration in anticipation of a climax. We braced for the attack, leaning forward as though into a wind.

And then something happened that I have never completely understood. Nothing was said; there was no signal, nor was there any break in the rhythm of our chanting. But suddenly all the women in our group—and the women made up more than half of the group's numbers—stepped out and surrounded the men;

their saris and kameezes became a thin, fluttering barrier, a wall around us. They turned to face the approaching men, challenging them, daring them to attack.

The thugs took a few more steps towards us and then faltered, confused. A moment later, they were gone.

~

The march ended at the walled compound where it had started. In the next couple of hours, an organization was created, the Nagrik Ekta Manch, or Citizens' Unity Front, and its work—to bring relief to the injured and the bereft, to shelter the homeless—began the next morning. Food and clothing were needed, and camps had to be established to accommodate the thousands of people with nowhere to sleep. And by the next day we were overwhelmed—literally. The large compound was crowded with vanloads of blankets, second-hand clothing, shoes, and sacks of flour, sugar, and tea. Previously hard-nosed unsentimental businessmen sent cars and trucks. There was barely room to move.

My own role was slight. For a few weeks, I worked with a team from Delhi University, distributing supplies in the slums and working-class neighbourhoods that had been worst hit by the rioting. Then I returned to my desk.

In time, inevitably, most of the Front's volunteers returned to their everyday lives. But some members—most notably the women involved in the running of refugee camps—continued to work for years afterwards with Sikh women and children who had been rendered homeless. Jaya Jaitley, Lalita Ramdas, Veena Das, Mita Bose, Radha Kumar: these women, each one an accomplished professional, gave up years of their time to repair the enormous damage that had been done in a matter of two or three days.

The Front also formed a team to investigate the riots. I briefly considered joining, but then decided that an investigation would be a waste of time because the politicians capable of inciting violence were unlikely to heed a tiny group of concerned citizens.

I was wrong. A document eventually produced by this team—a slim pamphlet entitled 'Who Are the Guilty?'—has become a classic, a searing indictment of the politicians who encouraged the riots and the police who allowed the rioters to have their way.

Over the years the Indian government has compensated some of the survivors of the 1984 violence and resettled some of the homeless. One gap remains: to this day, no instigator of the riots has been charged. But the pressure on the government has never gone away, and it continues to grow every year, the nails hammered in by that slim document dig just a little deeper.

The pamphlets and others that followed are testaments to the only humane possibility available to people who live in multi-ethnic, multi-religious societies like those of the Indian subcontinent. Human-rights documents such as 'Who Are the Guilty?' are essential to the process of broadening civil institutions: they are weapons with which society asserts itself against a state that runs criminally amok, as the one did in Delhi in November of 1984.

It is heartening that sanity prevails today in the Punjab. But not elsewhere. In Bombay, local government officials want to stop any public buildings from being painted green—a colour associated with the Muslim religion. And hundreds of Muslims have been deported from the city slums—in at least one case for committing an offence no graver than reading a Bengali newspaper. It is imperative that governments ensure that those who instigate mass violence do not go unpunished.

∽

The Bosnian writer Dzevad Karahasan, in a remarkable essay called 'Literature and War' (published in his collection *Sarajevo, Exodus of a City*), makes a startling connection between modern literary aestheticism and the contemporary world's indifference to violence: 'The decision to perceive literally everything as an aesthetic phenomenon—completely sidestepping questions about goodness and truth—is an artistic decision. That decision started in the realm of art, and went on to become characteristic of the contemporary world.'

When I went back to my desk in November of 1984, I found myself confronting decisions about writing that I had never faced before. How was I to write about what I had seen without reducing it to a mere spectacle? My next novel was bound to be influenced by my experiences, but I could see no way of writing directly about those events without recreating them as a panorama of violence—'an aesthetic phenomenon', as Karahasan was to call it. At the time, the idea seemed obscene and futile; of much greater importance were factual reports of the testimony of the victims. But these were already being done by people who were, I knew, more competent than I could be.

Within a few months, I started my novel, which I eventually called *The Shadow Lines*—a book that led me backward in time, to earlier memories of riots, ones witnessed in childhood. It became a book not about any one event but about the meaning of such events and their effects on the individuals who live through them.

And until now I have never really written about what I saw in November of 1984. I am not alone; several others who took part in that march went on to publish books, yet nobody, so far as I know, has ever written about it except in the passing.

There are good reasons for this, not least the politics of the situation, which leave so little room for the writer. The riots were generated by a cycle of violence, involving the terrorists in the Punjab on the one hand, and the Indian government on the other. To write carelessly in such a way as to endorse terrorism or repression, can add easily to the problem: in such incendiary circumstances, words cost lives, and it is only appropriate that those who deal in words should pay scrupulous attention to what they say. It is only appropriate that they should find themselves inhibited.

But there is also a simpler explanation. Before I could set down a word, I had to resolve a dilemma, between being a writer and being a citizen. As a writer, I had only one obvious subject: the violence. From the news report, or the latest film or novel, we have come to expect the bloody detail or the elegantly staged conflagration that closes a chapter or effects a climax. But it is worth asking if the very obviousness of this subject arises out of our modern conventions of representations; within the dominant aesthetic of our time—the aesthetic of what Karahasan calls 'indifference'—it is all too easy to present violence as an apocalyptic spectacle, while the resistance to it can as easily figure as mere sentimentality, or worse, as pathetic or absurd.

Writers don't join crowds—Naipaul and so many others teach us that. But what do you do when the constitutional authority fails to act? You join and in joining bear all the responsibilities and obligations and guilt that joining represents. My experience of the violence was overwhelmingly and memorably of the resistance to it. When I think of the women staring down the mob, I am not filled with a writerly wonder. I am reminded of my gratitude for being saved from injury. What I saw at first hand—and not merely on that march but on the bus, in Hari's house, in the huge compound that filled with essential goods—was not the horror of violence but the affirmation of humanity: in each case, I witnessed the risks that perfectly ordinary people were willing to take for one another.

When I now read descriptions of troubled parts of the world, in which violence appears primordial and inevitable, a fate to which masses of people are largely resigned, I find myself asking, Is that all there was to it? Or is it possible that the authors of these descriptions failed to find a form—or a style or a voice or a plot—that could accommodate both violence *and* the civilized, willed response to it?

The truth is that the commonest response to violence is one of repugnance and that a significant number of people everywhere try to oppose it in whatever ways they can. That these efforts rarely appear in accounts of violence is not surprising: they are too undramatic. For those who participate in them, they are often hard to write about for the very reasons that so long delayed my own account of 1984.

'Let us not fool ourselves,' Karahasan writes. 'The world is written first—the holy books say, that it was created in words—and all that happens in it, happens in language first.'

It is when we think of the world the aesthetic of indifference might bring into being that we recognize the urgency of remembering the stories we have not written.

TWO

~

THE FUNERAL*

RUSKIN BOND

'I don't think he should go,' said Aunt M.

'He's too small,' concurred Aunt B. 'He'll get upset and probably throw a tantrum. And you know Padre Lal doesn't like having children at funerals.'

The boy said nothing. He sat in the darkest corner of the darkened room, his face revealing nothing of what he thought and felt. His father's coffin lay in the next room, the lid fastened forever over the tired, wistful countenance of the man who had meant so much to the boy. Nobody else had mattered—neither uncles nor aunts nor the fond grandparents. Least of all the mother who was hundreds of miles away with another husband. He hadn't seen her since he was four—that was just over five years ago—and he did not remember her very well.

The house was full of people—friends, relatives,

*This story is taken from *Rhododendrons in the Mist: My Favourite Tales of the Himalaya* by Ruskin Bond, published by Aleph Book Company, 2019.

neighbours. Some had tried to fuss over him but had been discouraged by his silence, the absence of tears. The more understanding of them had kept their distance.

Scattered words of condolence passed back and forth like dragonflies on the wind. 'Such a tragedy!...' 'Only forty...' 'No one realized how serious it was...' 'Devoted to the child...'

It seemed to the boy that everyone who mattered in the hill station was present. And for the first time they had the run of the house for his father had not been a sociable man. Books, music, flowers, and his stamp collection had been his main preoccupations, apart from the boy.

A small hearse, drawn by a hill pony, was led in at the gate and several able-bodied men lifted the coffin and manoeuvred it into the carriage. The crowd drifted away. The cemetery was about a mile down the road and those who did not have cars would have to walk the distance.

The boy stared through a window at the small procession passing through the gate. He'd been forgotten for the moment—left in care of the servants, who were the only ones to stay behind. Outside it was misty. The mist had crept up the valley and settled like a damp towel on the face of the mountain. Everyone was wet although it hadn't rained.

The boy waited until everyone had gone and then he left the room and went out on the veranda. The gardener, who had been sitting in a bed of nasturtiums, looked up and asked the boy if he needed anything. But the boy shook his head and retreated indoors. The gardener, looking aggrieved because of the damage done to the flower beds by the mourners, shambled off to his quarters. The sahib's death meant that he would be out of a job very soon. The house would pass into other hands. The boy would go to an orphanage. There weren't many people who kept gardeners these days. In the kitchen, the cook was busy preparing the only big meal ever served in the house. All those relatives, and the padre too, would come back famished, ready for a sombre but nevertheless substantial meal. He, too, would be out of a job soon; but cooks were always in demand.

The boy slipped out of the house by a back door and made his way into the lane through a gap in a thicket of dog roses. When he reached the main road, he could see the mourners wending their way round the hill to the cemetery. He followed at a distance.

It was the same road he had often taken with his father during their evening walks. The boy knew the name of almost every plant and wildflower that grew on the hillside. These, and various birds and insects, had been described and pointed out to him by his father.

Looking northwards, he could see the higher ranges of the Himalaya and the eternal snows. The graves in the cemetery were so laid out that if their incumbents did happen to rise one day, the first thing they would see would be the glint of the sun on those snow-covered peaks. Possibly the site had been chosen for the view. But to the boy it did not seem as if anyone would be able to thrust aside those massive tombstones and rise from their graves to enjoy the view. Their rest seemed as eternal as the snows. It would take an earthquake to burst those stones asunder and thrust the coffins up from the earth. The boy wondered why people hadn't made it easier for the dead to rise. They were so securely entombed that it appeared as though no one really wanted them to get out.

'God has need of your father…' With those words a well-meaning missionary had tried to console him.

And had God, in the same way, laid claim to the thousands of men, women, and children who had been put to rest here in these neat and serried rows? What could he have wanted them for? Of what use are we to God when we are dead, wondered the boy.

The cemetery gate stood open but the boy leant against the old stone wall and stared down at the mourners as they shuffled about with the unease of a batsman about to face a very fast bowler. Only this bowler was invisible and would come up stealthily and from behind.

Padre Lal's voice droned on through the funeral service and then the coffin was lowered—down, deep down. The boy was surprised at how far down it seemed to go! Was that other, better world down in the depths of the earth? How could anyone, even a Samson, push his way back to the surface again? Superman did it in comics but his father was a gentle soul who wouldn't fight too hard against the earth and the grass and the roots of tiny trees. Or perhaps he'd grow into a tree and escape that way! 'If ever I'm put away like this,' thought the boy, 'I'll get into the root of a plant and then I'll become a flower and then maybe a bird will come and carry my seed away… I'll get out somehow!'

A few more words from the padre and then some of those present threw handfuls of earth over the coffin before moving away.

Slowly, in twos and threes, the mourners departed. The mist swallowed them up. They did not see the boy behind the wall. They were getting hungry.

He stood there until they had all gone. Then he noticed that the gardeners or caretakers were filling in the grave. He did not know whether to go forward or not. He was a little afraid. And it was too late now. The grave was almost covered.

He turned and walked away from the cemetery. The road stretched ahead of him, empty, swathed in mist. He was alone. What had his father said to him once? 'The strongest man in the world is he who stands alone.'

Well, he was alone, but at the moment he did not feel very strong.

For a moment he thought his father was beside him, that they were together on one of their long walks. Instinctively he put out his hand, expecting his father's warm, comforting touch. But there was nothing there, nothing, no one…

He clenched his fists and pushed them deep down into his

pockets. He lowered his head so that no one would see his tears. There were people in the mist but he did not want to go near them, for they had put his father away.

'He'll find a way out,' the boy said fiercely to himself. 'He'll get out somehow!'

THREE

~

PYRE*

AMITAVA KUMAR

My mother died in Patna on 7 January 2014. We cremated her two days later on the banks of the Ganga at Konhara Ghat near Patna, more than 150 miles downriver from the burning ghats of Benares where Hindus have cremated their dead since at least the middle of the first millennium BCE. I took notes. During the long fourteen-hour flight to India I dealt with my sorrow by writing in my notebook a brief obituary for a Hindi newspaper that Ma read each morning. I was paying tribute. But once I had arrived in Patna, my reasons for note-taking became more complicated. Grief makes you a stranger to yourself and I was struck by this person that I saw pierced with loss. I was taking notes so that I could remember who I was in those days following my mother's death.

*'Pyre' was published in *Granta* 130 and included in the *Best American Essays* edited by Jonathan Franzen, published by Houghton Mifflin Harcourt Publishing Company 2016.

In Ma's case, there was an inevitable delay. She had wanted me to be the one who lit her funeral pyre but I live in New York: I had boarded a direct flight to Delhi and then taken another plane to Patna. It was evening on the next day by the time I reached there. My family had tried to spare me from distress and hadn't told me that Ma had already died; but, unknown to them, before I left home I'd received a message on Facebook from a distant relative offering condolences. A large crowd stood in the dark outside our house and no one moved or spoke when I arrived. In the parlour-like space on the ground floor of our house, my father sat on a sofa with other males whom I didn't immediately recognize. I touched my father's feet and he said something about my luck in getting a quick connecting flight from Delhi. I stepped further inside. My two sisters were sitting on a mattress next to a metal box, their faces looking swollen; I embraced them and when I did that the other women in the room, seated on chairs pushed against the wall, began to wail.

A white sheet and strings of marigold covered the rectangular box, but at its foot the renting company had painted in large letters in Hindi: EST. 1967 PHONE 2219692. At first I thought the aluminium box was connected to an electrical outlet but later I found out that the box had space along its sides that had been packed with ice. A square glass window on its cover allowed a view of Ma's face. Her head was resting on a thin yellow pillow with a red flower print. Bits of cotton had been stuffed into her nostrils.

An older cousin took me to another room and told me that the cremation would be held the next morning. I was asked if I wanted to get my head shaved at the ghat just before the ceremony or if I'd prefer to visit a barber's in the morning and be spared the sting of the winter cold. I chose the latter. There could be no cooking fire in the house till the body had been cremated, and a simple vegetarian meal was brought from a relative's house. When most of the visitors had left for the night, my elder sister, whom I call Didi, said that the casket needed to be filled with fresh ice. A widowed aunt remarked that we should remove any jewellery from Ma because otherwise the Doms at the burning ghat, the men from the supposedly untouchable caste who built the pyre and were the custodians of the whole ceremony, would simply snatch it away. They didn't care, she said, and would just tear the flesh to rip off the gold. It was their right.

Ma's nose stud came off easily enough but the earrings were a problem. Her white hair was wrapped around the stud; using a pair of scissors I cut the hair but the earrings seemed stuck to the skin. My younger sister struggled with one of them, and I with the other. I didn't succeed and someone else had to complete the task. At one point, I found myself saying it was better to use surgical scissors right then so that we didn't have to watch Ma's ears torn by other hands. Didi said of the Doms, using an English term borrowed from her medical books, 'For them, it is just a *cadaver*.' I was unsettled but understood that the Doms were also reflecting an understanding that was drawn from deep within Hinduism: once the spirit has departed from the body, what remains is mere matter, no different from the log of wood on which it is placed. There was maybe a lesson in this for us, that we discard our squeamishness about death, but I felt a great tenderness as I looked down at my mother in that metal box. I caressed her cheeks. They felt cold to the touch, and slightly moist, as if even in death she had kept up her habit of applying lotion. A thin line of red fluid, like betel juice, glistened between her lips.

Having touched Ma's body, I also felt I should wash my hands. I went up to her room. Over the past couple of hours there had been the comfort of shared tears, but now I was alone for the first time. In the room where I had last seen my mother alive and quite well, only a few months earlier, her walking stick was leaning against the wall. Her saris, whose smell would have been familiar to me, hung in the cupboard. Next to the bed were the two pairs of her white sneakers equipped with Velcro straps for her arthritic hands. Standing in front of the bathroom sink, it occurred to me that the bar of Pears soap in the blue plastic dish was the one that Ma had put there just before she died. My first notes in Patna were about these items, which appeared to me like memorials that I knew would soon disappear.

My sisters and I slept that night on mattresses spread on the floor around the aluminium box. On waking up after perhaps four hours of sleep, I saw that my younger sister was awake, sitting quietly with her back to the wall, looking vacant and sad. Under the light of a bulb near a side door, visible through the glass, stood a man with a scarf wrapped around his head. It took me a minute to recognize him. He was from our ancestral village in Champaran and had been a servant in our house in Patna when I was a boy. He had travelled through the night with fresh bamboo that would be used to make the bier on which, according to custom, Ma's body would be carried out of the house and put on the funeral pyre.

When the sun came out after an hour, the rose bushes in the garden were only half visible through the fog, and the fog was still there on the water when we arrived at the river around noon.

That morning, while my sisters were washing Ma's body in preparation for the funeral, my father and I went to get our heads shaved. Papa asked the barber the name of his village; it turned out that the barber's village and ours were in the same district. My father knew a politician from the barber's village. The radio was playing Hindi songs. *Zulfein teri itni ghani, dekh ke inko, yeh sochta hoon… Maula mere Maula mere.* The barber was a small, dark man with a limp. He was extremely polite to my father, listening quietly while he talked about inflation and the changes in the economy. At one point, my father said that when he started life in Patna, he could buy a chicken for ten rupees and that now it would be difficult to get an egg for that amount.

I listened to what my father was saying with a rising sense of annoyance. I thought he was being pedantic when I wanted him to be sad—but why exactly? So that I could write down fragments of sentences in a little notebook? I began to see that Papa too was finding comfort by writing his own story of loss. There can be so much pathos in accounting. All the dumb confusion and wild fear of our lives rearranged in tidy rows in a ledger. One set of figures to indicate birth, and another set for death: the concerted attempt to repress the accidents and the pain of the period in between. Entire lives and accompanying histories of loss reduced to neat numbers. My father, with his phenomenal memory, was doing what he knew how to do best. He was saying to everyone in the room that everything had changed but the past was still connected to the present, if only through a narrative about changes in the price of eggs and chicken.

Ma's body had been taken out of the aluminium box by the time Papa and I returned home. Her fingernails and toenails were painted red. She was now draped in a pink Banarasi organza sari and a burgundy shawl with tiny silver bells and a shiny gold pattern of leaves. There were bright new bangles on her arm. Minutes before we left for the burning ghat, my father was brought into the room where Ma's adorned body lay on a stretcher on the floor. He was asked to put orange sindoor in the parting of Ma's hair, repeating the act he had performed on the day he married her. Papa was sobbing by now but he was asked to repeat the gesture thrice. Then all the women in the family, many of them weeping loudly, took turns rubbing the auspicious powder in Ma's hair.

When we were in the car, driving to the Ganga for the cremation, Didi said that my mother was lucky. At her death, Ma had been dressed up in new clothes. Papa had put sindoor on her head, signifying that they were getting married again. Ma was going out as a bride. Had my father died first, none of this would have happened. If Ma were still living, sindoor would have been wiped away from her head. She would be expected to wear white. The women from the family who were now wailing would still be wailing but, if Ma were the widow, these women would have had the task of breaking all the bangles on her wrist before Papa's corpse was taken out of the house.

As I listened to my sister, I understood that even in the midst of profound grief it was necessary to find comfort. One needed solace. It was possible to hold despair at bay by imagining broken bangles and the destiny that my mother had escaped. I would have found the sight of my mother's bare arms unbearable.

I left India nearly three decades ago, and would see my mother only for a few days each year during my visits to Patna. Over the past ten or fifteen years, her health had been declining. She suffered from arthritis and the medicines she took for it had side effects, and sometimes my phone rang with news that she'd fallen asleep in the bathroom or had a seizure on the morning after she had fasted during a festival. I knew that one day the news would be worse and I would be asked to come to Patna. I was fifty years old and had never before attended a funeral. I didn't know what was more surprising, that some of the rituals were new to me, or that they were exactly as I had imagined. That my mother's corpse had been dressed as a bride was new and disconcerting, and I'd have preferred a plainer look; on the other hand, the body placed on the bamboo bier, its canopy covered with an orange sheet of cotton, was a familiar daily sight on the streets of my childhood. In my notebook that night I noted that my contribution to the funeral had been limited to lighting my mother's funeral pyre. In more ways than one, the rituals of death had reminded me that I was an outsider. There were five hundred people at the shraadh dinner. I only knew a few of them. I wouldn't have known how to make arrangements for the food or the priests. Likewise, for the shamiana, the community hall where the dinner was held, the notice in the newspapers about the shraadh, even the chairs on which the visitors sat.

There is a remarkable short story by A. K. Ramanujan called

'Annayya's Anthropology' in which the Kannada protagonist, a graduate student at the University of Chicago, makes a terrible discovery while looking at a book in the library. The book is by an American anthropologist whose fieldwork had been done in India; the pictures in the book from Annayya's home town appear familiar to him. One of the photographs illustrates a Hindu cremation and Annayya recognizes in the crowd a cousin who owns a photography studio. This is a picture that appears to have been taken in Annayya's own home in Mysore. The cousin, whose name is Sundararaya, is mentioned in the book's foreword. When Annayya looks more carefully at the corpse in the photograph he sees that it is his father on the pyre. Ramanujan was making a point about the discipline of anthropology, about the ironies of our self-discoveries in the mirror of Western knowledge, but the story tugs at the immigrant's dread that distance will prevent his fulfilment of filial duty.

I had been luckier than Annayya. I had been able to speak to Didi in Patna when Ma was taken to a hospital on the night she died. On WhatsApp, on my phone, a text came from my sister later in the evening, assuring me that Ma was doing better. Then came the call about my flight timings. While the use of social media meant that I got the news of my mother's death from a near stranger on Facebook, it was also true that technology and modern travel had made it quite easy for me to arrive in Patna in less than twenty hours to cremate my mother. During the prayer ceremonies a priest told me that the reason Hindu customs dictated a mourning period of thirteen days was that it used to take time for all the relatives to be informed and for them to travel to the home of the deceased. But this, he said, putting his hand on his ear, is the age of the mobile phone.

At the ghat, the smoke from the funeral fires mixed with the lingering fog of the winter afternoon. An advance party organized by a cousin's husband had pitched a small shamiana on the bank and arranged a few red plastic chairs next to it. Above the din, a tuneless bhajan played on a loudspeaker. In the crowd, I was led first in one direction and then another. My movements were restrained because of what I was wearing; according to custom, my body was wrapped in two pieces of unstitched cotton. My freshly shaven head was bare. I saw that Ma's body had already been put on the pyre. There was such a press of strangers, many of them beggars and curious children, that I had to ask people loudly to move back. Ma lay on heavy logs and a bed of straw but the priest directed me to pile thinner firewood over the rest of the body. Other family members joined me, adding sticks in the shape of a tent over the corpse.

Ma's face had been left bare. Now the priest told me to put five pieces of sandalwood near my mother's mouth. Some of the sindoor that had been put in Ma's hair had scattered and lodged in her eyebrows and on her eyelids. The Dom who would give me the fire had an X-shaped plaster stuck on his right cheek. He had a dark face and his eyes were bloodshot. His head was wrapped in a brown-and-blue muffler to protect him from the cold; he wore jeans and a thin black jacket and he had about him an air of insouciance that would have bothered my mother, but I liked him. His presence was somehow reassuring, or real, because he was outside the circle of our grief and yet the main doer. He was solemn, but he certainly wasn't sober; his very casualness brought a quotidian touch to the scene, and he accentuated this by haggling about his payment. A maternal uncle's son stood behind me, repeating for my benefit the priest's instructions—this cousin of mine, a few years older than I, had cremated his son recently. The boy had passed away after his liver stopped working, the result of an allergic reaction to medicines that have reportedly been banned outside India. The priest told me to sprinkle *gangajal* again—the endless act of purification with what is in reality polluted water—before the Dom lit a bundle of tall straw for me. Three circles around the pyre. Then followed the ritual that is called *mukhaagni*. I understood suddenly why the priest had given me the five pieces of sandalwood, the size of small Snickers bars, to put near my mother's mouth. In that moment, while performing *mukhaagni* inadequately, inefficiently, even badly, in my grief and bewilderment, the thought passed through my mind: Is this why my mother had wanted me present at her death? *Mukhaagni*—in Sanskrit, *mukha* is 'mouth' and *agni* is 'fire'—means in practice that the male who is closest to the deceased, often the son, sometimes the father, and in some cases, I imagine, the husband, puts fire into the mouth of the person on the pyre.

A cremation on a riverbank in India is by its very nature public, but usually the only mourners present are men. In our case, my sisters and other younger women from the family had accompanied Ma's body. When I turned from the pyre I saw my sisters standing at the edge of the circle. I went to them and put my arms around their shoulders. The flames had risen at once and they hid Ma's body behind an orange curtain. Soon there were fewer people standing around the pyre and the older men, my father's friends, began to settle down on the plastic chairs at a distance of about thirty feet from the pyre. A relative put a shawl around me. Then the Dom said that the fire was burning too quickly, meaning that the fire would go out before the corpse had been incinerated, so a few men from our party took down a part of the shamiana and used it as a screen against the wind.

The fire needed to burn for three hours. Badly managed fires and, sometimes, the plain paucity of firewood—for the pyre requires at least 150 kilos of wood but often as much as four hundred kilos or more—are to be blamed for the partially charred torsos flung into the Ganga. And as wood costs money—10,000 rupees in our case—the poor in particular can be insufficiently burned. The chief minister of Bihar, Jitan Ram Manjhi, a man from the formerly untouchable Musahar (or rat-eating) caste, told an audience in Patna last year that his family was so poor that when his grandfather died they just threw his body into the river.

I asked Didi why we hadn't taken Ma's body to Patna's electric crematorium, but she only said that Ma wouldn't have wanted it. Didi didn't need to say anything else. I could imagine my mother resisting the idea of being put in a metal tray where other bodies had been laid and pushed inside an oven where electric coils would reduce her to ashes. Her choice, superstitious and irrational as it might be, didn't pose a problem for us. We could afford the more expensive and customary means of disposing of the dead. Nearly three hundred kilos of wood had been purchased for Ma's pyre and, in addition to that, ten kilos of sandalwood. This was one of the many instances during those days when I recognized that we were paying for the comfort of subscribing to tradition. The electric crematorium is often the choice of the poor, costing only about three hundred rupees. I learned that over seven hundred dead are cremated at the electric crematorium at Patna's Bans Ghat each month, and a somewhat smaller number at the more distant Gulbi Ghat electric crematorium. These numbers are only a fraction of the three thousand cremated on traditional pyres at Bans Ghat on average each month. This despite the fact that electric cremation is also quicker, taking only forty-five minutes, except when there is a long wait due to power cuts. There can also be other delays. Back when I was in college, the corpse of a relative of mine, a sweet old lady with a fondness for betel leaf, was taken to the Patna crematorium, but the operator there said that he would be available only after he had watched that day's broadcast of the TV serial *Ramayan*. The mourners waited an extra hour.

While we sat under the shamiana watching the fire do its work, my younger sister Dibu said that she had put perfume on Ma's corpse because fragrances were something Ma liked. Dibu began to talk about how Ma used to put perfume in the new handkerchiefs that she gave away to younger female relatives who visited her. In Bihar, a Hindu woman leaving her home is given a handkerchief with a few grains of rice, a pinch of turmeric, leaves of grass, coins and a sweet laddoo. These items had also been put beside Ma on the pyre, and, I now learned, inside Ma's mouth my sisters had placed a gold leaf. I thought of the priest telling me each time I completed a circle around the pyre that I was to put the fire into my mother's mouth. I didn't, or couldn't. It wasn't so much that I found it odd or appalling that such a custom should exist; instead, I remember being startled that no one had cared to warn me about it. But perhaps I shouldn't have been. Death provided a normalizing context for everything that was being done. No act appeared outlandish because it had a place in the tradition, each Sanskrit verse carrying an intonation of centuries of practice. And if there was any doubt about the efficacy of sacred rituals, everywhere around us banal homilies were being offered to make death appear less strange or devastating. The bhajan that had been playing on the loudspeaker all afternoon was in praise of fire. *Death, you think you have defeated us, but we sing the song of burning firewood.* Even though it was tuneless, and even tasteless, the song turned cremation into a somewhat celebratory act. It struck me that the music disavowed its own macabre nature and made everything acceptable. And now, as the fire burned lower and there was visibly less to burn, I saw that everyone, myself included, had momentarily returned to a sense of the ordinary. This feeling wouldn't last more than a few hours but at that time I felt free from the contagion of tears. I remember complaining about the loud music. Everyone had been fasting since morning and pedas from a local confectioner were taken out of paper boxes. I took a box of pedas to our young Dom but he refused; he didn't want anything sweet to eat. I was handed a packet of salted crackers to pass on to him. Tea was served in small plastic cups. Street dogs and goats wandered past the funeral pyres. Broken strings of marigold, fruit peels and bits of bedding, including blankets and a pillow pulled from the fire, littered the sandy bank. One of my uncles had lost his car keys and people from our group left to look for them.

The Dom had so far used a ten-foot-long bamboo to rearrange the burning logs but when the fire died down he poked around the burning embers with his calloused fingers. I was summoned for another round of prayers and offerings to the fire. The men in my family gave directions to the Dom as he scooped Ma's remains—ash and bones, including a few vertebrae, but other small bones too, white and curiously flat—into a large earthen pot. This pot was wrapped in red cloth and later that evening hung from a high branch on the mango tree outside our house. Its contents were to be immersed in the Ganga at the holy sites upriver: Benares, Prayag and Haridwar. This was a journey my sisters and I would undertake later in the week; but that afternoon, after the pot had been filled, the rest of the half-burnt wood and ash and what might have been a part of the hip bone were flung into the river while the priest chanted prayers. Flower petals, mostly marigold, had been stuffed in polythene bags which had the names of local sari shops printed on them, and at the end everyone took part in casting handfuls of bright petals on the brown waters. I took pictures. The photograph of the yellow marigold floating on the Ganga, rather than my mother's burning pyre, is what I put up on Facebook that evening.

FOUR

~

SEED*

MAHASWETA DEVI

Translated from the Bengali by Ipshita Chanda

The land north of Kuruda and Hesadi villages is uneven, and so arid and sun-baked that there is not a hint of grass even after the rains. You might see the occasional erect serpent hoods of cactus plants, and a few neem trees. In the middle of this scorched wasteland, where no cattle graze, is a low-lying, boat-shaped piece of land. Around half a bigha. You can spot this bit of land only if you climb a high embankment; the splash of green, from the wild aloe bushes that grow on the land, presents an eerie sight.

Even more sinister is the machan in the middle of the field, a platform on wooden posts topped by a thatched hut. A hut on the land is most unsettling for anyone who sees it, because such a hut is generally built to guard crops. Only stray aloe plants grow here, with leaves as

*This story is taken from *Tell Me a Long, Long Story: 12 Memorable Stories from India* edited by Mini Krishnan, published by Aleph Book Company, 2017.

thorny as the plant of the pineapple. Even buffaloes don't eat them. Elsewhere in the world, the fibre from these plants makes extremely strong ropes. In India, they are dismissed as wild bushes.

The most eerie scene occurs as evening falls. A man comes striding along from Kuruda village. As he approaches, you can see that he's old, his skin gnarled and knotted, a loincloth wrapped around his waist, a quilted bag hanging from it. He carries a stick and raps the aloe plants at random as he approaches the machan. He climbs the rickety ladder fastened to the branches of the tree. He strikes a flint stone, lights a beedi and sits down on the machan. Every day. When night falls, he spreads a mat and goes to sleep. Every night.

At this time, every day, in Kuruda village, the old wife of Dulan Ganju yells curses at him. This is her right. Because this old man is Dulan Ganju. Her son, daughter-in-law, and grandchildren dislike this yelling and cursing, but can't do anything about it. If they protest, they'll be abused too. And in these parts, Dhatua's mother's abusive powers are legendary. In every dispute, she is called upon to exhibit her professional squabbling skills. She takes the field and starts by cursing the first of the adversary's seven previous generations. Generally, by the time she reaches the third generation, the opposition flees the field.

She is widely respected. When there was trouble at Tamadih during the Emergency, the police had come to this village asking questions. Dhatua's mother's fiery tongue had forced them to leave. One of the fugitives the police was seeking was hiding in the loft of the cowshed. Dhatua's mother's strident commands to 'Come, search every room, you vultures!' conclusively proved that the whole village was completely innocent.

She didn't stop there. 'Look,' she said, 'there are only children and the elderly in the village. Want to examine them? Want to arrest them?'

Once the police left, Dhatua's mother bloodied the fugitive with her sharp tongue, 'Rotoni! You've always been a halfwit!

Less sense than a nanny goat! So you axed a Rajput mahajan? Excellent, well done. You should've despatched the devil by giving it to him in the neck. Why didn't you hide in the jungle? Which idiot returns to his village? Go, go to the forest!'

Dhatua and Latua don't have the guts to tell their mother, 'Don't curse our baba.'

If they do, Ma will explode. So, the old man is now his sons' darling, and their mother a worthless old she-goat! Do the sons know their father's true character? Only she knows.

Ma had been married at the age of four. At fourteen, after the gaona ceremony when she attained puberty, she made her husband's family her home. Ma knew the old man through and through. Lord of a thorny wasteland, guarding his land alone. After all, who would be widowed if a snake bit him or a tiger dragged him off? Dhatua and Latua? Could they fool the government into giving them seeds every year for that barren piece of land? Collect government fertilizer and sell it off? Extract money from the government for the maintenance of a plough and buffalo borrowed from the pahaan, the village priest, year after year?

The sons fall silent. Ma puffs away at her hookah and, delivering her final, unanswerable line, 'You'll never know my true worth till I'm dead,' goes off to sleep. The daughters-in-law whisper to the sons, 'Well, another day gone.'

Ma addresses the darkness, 'One day he'll lie there dead. I won't even be here.'

The sons know it is abnormal to guard the aloe plants every night. But they don't consider their father a normal person by any standards. Baba is a dark character, complicated and impossible to understand. The trade of the Ganju caste is skinning dead animals. Baba poisoned a few buffaloes that belonged to the powerful Rajput mahajan, Lachman Singh, owner of ten rifles. This in Lachman Singh's own village, Tamadih. Then he sold the skins. Characteristically, Lachman suspected his traditional rival, his brother and co-heir Daitari Singh of the crime. The resultant family feud is still raging.

Despite this, Baba survives, proving that he is a man of a different measure. Always busy with such strategies of survival, he had never had time for his sons or grandsons.

Ma is no less. Her mature old bones have such stamina, bear such stubborn courage and resentment, that she, too, is beyond the ordinary measure of a human being.

Their sons had never seen their father and mother seated together chatting. But when Baba is planning something important, he asks Ma to come and sit in the courtyard. Lights her hookah and says, 'Eh Dhatuake ma! Advise me. Give me your advice. Everyone in the village consults you, even the police are scared of you.'

'What mischief are you brewing now? Who're you planning to cheat or rob?'

Ma's voice is loud, but without rancour. Together they plot and plan in low voices. Such an event occurs once a year or every year-and-a-half.

At other times, Baba doesn't pay any attention to Ma. She says, 'I might as well go back to my father's house.'

Baba smiles slyly and quietly tells the breeze, 'Yes. To that huge mansion of your father's in Tura village.'

Ma has no father-mother-brothers. Yet she gives Baba the opportunity to smile crookedly and pass mocking remarks.

This is what Latua and Dhatua's parents are like—and there's nothing to be done about it. Just as you can't help the fact that the hill lies to the west, or that the Kuruda River flows nearby. Sanichari says, 'Your father and mother are both mad. Your father, of course, is completely crazy. Why else would he guard that land without ever farming it? Why?'

There's a proverb which says that what you pick up free is worth fourteen annas. The land was free, but there wasn't even fourteen paise profit from it.

The land belongs to Lachman Singh. Quite a few years ago,

activists belonging to the Sarvodaya movement, which sought to redistribute land from the rich to the poor, had gone from door to door to every landlord in this area. About them too, Sanichari used to say, 'These are madmen of the babu caste. They'll make the landlords feel deep regret and spontaneously admit, "Tch, tch! We have so much land, and they have none at all?" And they'll give away the land. The day they do this, I'll sit on a divan, eat butter and cream, and cook rice twice a day.'

But some landlords did begin to give away little bits of stony, barren land to provoke their fellow landlords into doing the same. Everyone had 500 or 700 or 1,000 or 2,000 bighas of fertile land. Everyone harvested paddy or maize or maroa or mustard or arhar. Groundnuts earned large profits. So it didn't really matter much if you gave away some land.

The Sarvodaya leaders and workers had become the butt of their countrymen's mockery. The gifts of land saved their face. Didn't the upper-caste Rajput and Kayastha mahajans, jotedars who owned or controlled the land in the Kuruda belt give up their lands? Didn't that mean they had had a change of heart? Certainly. Bas. The Sarvodaya mission was successful. Immediately after this, the activists would go off to change the hearts of the dacoits in Madhya Pradesh. Their mission would not be complete till they filled the hearts of two classes—the landlords and the dacoits—with remorse.

The gifting of land has many uses. It is a way of getting rid of barren land and buying over its recipients. It strengthens one's position with the government. Above all, like a rasgulla after a meal, there is the added satisfaction of knowing one is compassionate.

Dulan Ganju gets this land. He didn't want to take it. But Lachman Singh is too powerful. His eyes grew red with anger and he said, 'Typical of you low castes! Today I'm feeling generous, so I'm giving you this. Fool, do you think I'll feel this way tomorrow?'

Dulan said, 'Hujoor is my mai-baap.'

'Then? Low-lying-land floods every monsoon, sow whatever you like and you'll get high yields.'

During the monsoons, reddish water streams down the embankment and collects in the field. But all around lay barren, stony ground. Who'll go all that way to plough that land? If it was fertile land, would Lachman Singh have let it lie fallow? Dulan had gone to borrow money. He came back a landlord.

Everyone in the village said, 'It's a rich man's whim! He eats parathas soaked in ghee, and the heat's gone to his head. He'll forget all about it tomorrow.'

'Suppose he doesn't?'

'Just let the land be. In Ara-Chhapra, this is the kind of land they gave at the behest of the Sarvodayis. Those who got it sold it back to the mahajan or mortgaged it to him. You'll do the same.'

'Who'll take that land? The mahajan's buying himself a good name, and at the same time getting rid of it.'

Dulan would have said more, but the pahaan who was part of his audience gave him a mighty tongue-lashing. People had so many problems to deal with, what was Dulan's land trouble in comparison?

Dulan mutters and grumbles.

His wife says, 'Oh! He's busy calculating how to make a profit from this land, but just look at the fuss he's making! No one's ever seen through his wiles.'

'Profit from the land?'

The next day, Sanichari hears all about it and says, 'Why? Eh, Dhatuakemaiya! If he gets land, Dhatuakebaap can go to Tohri! To the block development office! The government will bear the expenses of farming, seeds, everything!'

Only when he heard this did Dulan smile. His eyes glazed over with dreams. Even a man like Dulan had not realized how barren land could help him run his household. In some fairy tales, cows yield milk even though they haven't calved.

~

One day, the land came into Dulan's possession in the form of documents and deeds. They had two adjacent rooms and a corridor in the Ganju neighbourhood: rooms that served as a living room, kitchen, everything. This was his world. Barricaded, one end of the corridor turned into a bedroom for husband and wife. Someone so bereft of support generally has no backbone. All around him were Rajput jotedars and mahajans; the Brahman priest Hanuman Misra of Tahar was particularly influential in these parts. Living in such an area, continuously under the thumb of the higher castes, would naturally break the spirit of people like Dulan who belonged to the lower Ganju and Dusadh castes.

But the drive for survival prompted him to exploit situations by using his natural guile rather than force. He fooled his powerful adversaries not by strength, but by wit and cunning. All the stratagems of survival were at his fingertips.

Dhatua's mother says, 'It's a large piece of land, very fertile. Oh, Dhatua, tell your baba to build a granary for his crops. Oh, Latua-re, your father's become a zamindar, yes, a zamindar!'

She said all this, but the villagers and she continued to wait to see what Dulan would do.

The villagers were appreciative witnesses to Dulan's one-man strategic warfare. Everyone knew about the business of Lachman Singh's buffaloes, but no one told on Dulan. He sold a pumpkin to Daitari Singh's household and took money from both Daitari's wife and mother. When the bananas and radishes were brought in a bullock cart from Lachman Singh's house to the banks of the Kuruda River during the Chhat festival, he walked beside the cart, shooing away imaginary birds, and continuously stealing things. Not once had he ever given a single thing to the other villagers. Yet, they treated him with respect. He could do what they dared not do.

As soon as he got the land, Dulan touched Lachman Singh's

knees and said, 'Malik, protector! You've given me land, but how will I farm it? I won't get a thing from the BD office. A-ha-ha, such a good piece of land! I've got it, but I can't use it.'

'Why? The BD office will give you everything.'

'No, hujoor, I'm a low caste.'

'Of course you are. It's because you don't remember this that you get kicked around. Sure, you're a low caste! But how can they refuse to help someone *I'm* giving land to? Who's the BD babu?'

'Kayastha, hujoor. Says the Rajputs are stupid country bumpkins. Listens to the radio all the time and uses his left hand to drink water, tea.'

'Arre Ram Ram! Chee, chee, chee.'

'I've seen it myself, hujoor.'

'I'll write to him.'

Lachman Singh is no learned mahapundit. He keeps a vakil. The vakil writes a strong appeal in Kayathi* Hindi advocating that Dulan get money in instalments to buy a plough and bullock, seeds and fertilizer. The BDO might live in Tohri, and it's true that Tohri is far from Lachman's village, Tamadih, but he has only one life. The SDO himself has warned him to avoid conflicts with Lachman and Hanuman Misra. So he immediately agreed to everything. He explained to the loincloth-clad Dulan in a very gentle voice that he would get seeds and fertilizer. But he wouldn't get the entire amount for the plough and bullock at one go. If he could pay an advance and show that he had bought the plough and bullock, he would get the rest of the money.

Dulan returned to the village and said to the pahaan, 'The sarkar makes laws, but doesn't understand anything. People buy ploughs and bullocks with cash. Who will sell to someone who pays in instalments? Lend me your plough and bullock.'

Dulan got the money by displaying that plough and bullock

---

*Local variant of Hindi, used for legal documents.

every alternate year. Every time he asks the BDO for the money, he says, 'The bullock died, hujoor.'

He takes the money. Collects the fertilizer and sells it at Tohri itself. Hoists the sack of seeds onto his shoulder and brings it home.

He eats the seeds.

It's no easy task to boil paddy seeds and make rice. But he does it. The first time, his wife had said, 'So much seed! How much land do you have?'

'You can't measure it even if you try.'

'What do you mean?'

'Our hunger. Can hunger be measured? The land of the stomach keeps expanding! You want me to farm that barren strip of land? Are you crazy?'

'What'll you do, then?'

'Boil it, grind it, we'll eat it.'

'Are you going to kill yourself eating seeds?'

'We haven't died yet. Didn't we eat rats during the famine? Why should we die from eating seeds? If we do, at least we'll have died eating rice! We'll go to heaven.'

It took Dhatua's mother just one meal of rice made from the seeds to realize that she had never eaten anything so sweet in her life.

She proudly told everyone in the village about this tasty food. Can any other married woman in the village boast of how brainy her man is, of how cunningly he fooled the gorment so that his family could eat paddy-rice seeds?

Everyone in the village was pleased. The gorment has never protected their interests. The gorment's BDO never helps them with farming. Their children never get to enter the gorment's primary school. Lachman Singh or Daitari Singh force them to harvest their crops for four annas a day or a single meal, at gunpoint. There was a lot of tension over this, because the Ganjus-Dusadhs-Dhobis of the neighbouring block were getting kicked and fed for eight annas daily. The villagers wanted a raise of twenty-five paise. Knowing all this, whenever there was trouble, the SDO brought in police reinforcements and picked up the labourers. Lachman Singh and Daitari were let off without a word.

The gorment belongs to Lachman Singh. The gorment belongs to Lachman Singh, Daitari Singh, Hanuman Misra. If such a gorment is fleeced by someone who happens to be a Dulan Ganju, then the villagers are bound to appreciate it.

Like the mythical Kaamdhenu, the cow that never ceased giving, the land continues to yield Dulan about six hundred rupees annually. But Dulan continued to sleep outdoors. At the corner of the covered veranda, on a platform beside Dhatua's mother, who coughs and wheezes as if she has asthma. They tie a billy goat beneath the platform when they go to sleep. A son to a room, each with his wife and children. Wheat, maroa, corncobs by the sackful, pots and pans, firewood, everything stacked in the same room. The earnings from the land cannot see them through the whole year, so father and sons work as field labourers, or search the forest for wild potatoes, or carry headloads in Tohri, or work in Misraji's orchards. Like everyone else.

One day, Karan Dusadh of Tamadih arrived in the village. A glamorous personality who used to work as a labourer in Lachman's field. He had a dispute over wages with the owner-manager, the malik, and went to jail at Hazaribagh where he made friends with prisoners from other parts of Bihar. They didn't shrink from him because he was a low-caste Dusadh. They respected him as a fighter. They were amazed that with no organizational help at all, 200 labourers had turned against an ocean of exploitation and set fire to the powerful Lachman Singh's fields of ripened wheat. They explained to him the importance of battles like theirs, burgeoning everywhere. The need to fight in an organized way. The need to fight from their own base.

The repercussions were swift and merciless. They were tortured. They were beaten up by the authorities. Many were even beaten to death. Despite all this, they told Karan, 'You're a fighter, you did the right thing, never give up the fight.'

Hence, there was turmoil in the layers of Karan Dusadh's mind. The Karan who had rebelled only when Lachman Singh had driven him to the end of his tether, now came out of jail and said to everyone, 'Conditions are unchanged. Why wait till he forces us to resist, get shot at, get jailed? Let's organize in advance. Talk things over with him. Ask the police to be present during harvesting. Our demands are very few. We're Harijans and Adivasis. We won't get good wages in these parts. We'll fight for eight annas. Women-men-children, eight annas for everyone. He's giving four annas. This will be our "twenty-five-paise battle" for an additional four annas.'

As soon as Dulan heard about this, he called Karan to Kuruda. Suspicious by nature, he insisted they talk on the embankment at the edge of his land, away from everyone. Karan Dusadh is middle-aged, scrawny, a tiny man. After two years with the prisoners in Hazaribagh, he is like a new person.

'All this caste business is rubbish. It's the Brahman and the wealthy who have spun these tales about untouchability.'

His words startle Dulan. For a moment he is speechless. Then—he's an old fox, after all!—'Oh, the babus who can read and write have always said that. Now let's get down to business. That Lachman Singh and the BDO, SDO and daroga, the police chief, drink together. First, go to the Adivasi office and the Harijan Seva Sangh at Tohri. Keep them informed. Let them go with you to the thana and the SDO.'

'Why? Are we that weak?'

'Yes, we are, Karan. Make no mistake. The entire sarkar will help Lachman. He can open fire and they won't notice. But you raise a stick and they'll catch you. Madanlalji of the Harijan Seva Sangh is a good man. Everyone knows him. Get him to back you.'

Karan takes this advice. Madanlal can garner a powerful pool of votes. So the SDO and daroga secretly consult with Lachman

Singh. Then they agree to what Madanlal says.

The harvesting and gathering of the corn go on without incident. Eight annas as wages. Karan Dusadh becomes a hero. A fairy tale come true.

Then, abruptly, Lachman tells Dulan, 'Stay on your land tomorrow. If anyone gets to know that I've told you this, I'll kill you.'

When this 'tomorrow' turns into 'today' at daybreak, the SDO suddenly goes off to Ranchi and the daroga to far-off Purudiha, chasing bandits.

As evening turns to dusk, in the radiance of the setting sun, Lachman Singh, accompanied by his Rajput-caste brothers, attacks the Dusadh quarters in Tamadih.

Fires rage, people burn, huts collapse.

~

At night, the newly risen moon reveals an unearthly silent scene before Dulan's eyes. Lachman Singh on horseback. Two horses tied abreast, a plank across their backs, laden with two corpses. Ten of Lachman's men escort the landlord.

At the point of Lachman's gun, Dulan buries Karan and his peaceable brother, Bulaki, in his land. Terrified, head bowed, he digs deep holes with his shovel. Lachman stands on the edge of the field, supervising and chewing paan. Then he says, 'Breathe a word of this to anyone, you cur, and you'll join Karan Dusadh. We can't trust the jackals and wolves not to dig up the corpses. Build a machan here tomorrow. Stay on guard at night. I'm the son of a Rajput! Karan lit this fire—from now on, there'll be more dead bodies.'

Dulan nods. In order to survive, he says, 'As you wish.'

The police came the next day to investigate the attack. A lot of hullabaloo. Ultimately it was learnt that Karan wasn't even present during the disturbance; the reporters' attempts to write 'A True Harijan Story' at all costs were totally foiled. No one said a word against Lachman Singh. One of his henchmen spent a few days in jail for arson. The government gave a pittance in compensation to those rendered homeless for the construction of new huts.

From then on, Dulan sleeps on the land. At first, this is seen as a sign of insanity, and his sons try to dissuade him. No advice penetrates Dulan's ears at this stage. When questioned, he glowers silently at them with bloodshot eyes. Then, shaking his head, he threatens them with his stick, 'Don't talk to me, Dhatua! I'll break your head.'

~

A great explosion, a landslide, occurs in the strata of his mind, ending in mental upheaval. So easy! Is everything so easy for the Lachmans? Dulan had thought that just as a man's life is linked to so many rites and rituals, so is his death. But Lachman Singh has proved that these time-honoured customs are meaningless. How easy! Two corpses on horseback! And these corpses must have been carried off arrogantly, from right under the Tamadih Dusadhs's noses. Lachman knows there's no need to hide them. Witnesses won't say a thing. They have read the warning in Lachman's sharp, silent gaze. He who opens his mouth will die. This has happened before. And will happen again. Once in a while it is necessary to rend the sky with leaping flames and the screams of the dying, just to remind the Harijans and untouchables that government laws, appointments of officers and constitutional decrees are nothing. Rajputs remain Rajputs, Brahmans remain Brahmans and Dusadh-Chamar-Ganju-Dhobi remain lower than Brahman-Kayastha-Rajput-Bhumihar-Kurmi. The Rajput or Brahman or Kayastha or Bhumihar or Yadav or Kurmi is, in places, as poor as, or even poorer than, the Harijan. But they are not tossed into the flames because of their caste. The fire god, having tasted the flesh of forest-dwelling, black-skinned outcastes during the burning of the Khandav forest,* is fond of the taste of the untouchable poor.

All this causes havoc in Dulan's mind. Before this, his was a surface cunning. Aimed at survival. Now he has to conceal two corpses beneath his heart. They begin to rot within him. Buried in the earth, Karan and Bulaki grow lighter as they gradually lose the burden of flesh. But in the realm of Dulan's mind, the corpses weigh heavy. He looks wan, hardly speaks. He can't confide in anyone. The constant burden he bears makes him feel as if he is tied to a whipping post. If he opens his mouth, the Dusadh quarters of Kuruda will go up in flames, ashes will scatter in the air, along with the stench of charred flesh.

Slowly time passes. Everyone is forced to forget that two people, Karan and Bulaki, went missing. From Tohri to Burudiha on one side and Phuljhar on the other, rail tracks are laid. According to area and jurisdiction, the thana and the SDO are given special powers to immediately investigate, take action, prepare cases for court, in instances of atrocities against Adivasis and Harijans. A panchayati well is dug in Dhai village. Dhai is a lower caste and Adivasi village. In this fashion, the area attempts to limp towards modernity.

The result of all this is to make Lachman Singh more powerful. He pooh-poohs government dictates and pays field labourers forty paise as wages, gifts a golden cobra to crown the Shiva idol in Hanuman Misra's temple, buys the BDO a scooter and the daroga a transistor radio, and takes over the bigha-and-a-half of land belonging to Karan and Bulaki as repayment of an old loan.

Everyone accepts all this. But all at once, there is a government circular about field labourers and with it comes a new SDO. This man is suspected of being left of centre, and because it is the administration's pious intention to drive the final nail into his coffin and suspend him, he is transferred to Tohri one-and-a-half

---

*Forest in the Mahabharata

months before the harvesting season begins.

The field labourers in the Tohri area are Harijans and Adivasis. The landowners, jotedars and mahajans, are upper caste. The particular problem of the area is the deep distrust of the labourers for the masters. This explains the lack of progress in agriculture or increase in individual incomes. Income, expenditure, health, education, social consciousness, everything continues to remain at a sub-normal level. An enlightened, sympathetic, humane officer is needed here.

The SDO realizes that he's in deep trouble. He tells his father-in-law, you win. Look for a bank job for me. I'm a student of Afro-economics, I might even get it. Else, where they're sending me, your only daughter will definitely end up a widow.

Having made alternative job arrangements, the SDO tells the impatient field labourers, 'You have the right to get five rupees eighty paise as wages.' He officially informs the jotedars of this. Lachman Singh's land and crop and labourers are spread over a vast area, including villages like Tamadih, Burudiha, Kuruda, Hesadi, Chama and Dhai. The son of the Burudiha village headman, Asrafi Mahato, says, 'We still remember Karan. We haven't forgotten him these three years. But this SDO is a good man. Why should we harvest crops for just forty paise and a meal? Five rupees eighty paise! We don't want the meal, let him give us five rupees forty paise as total wages.'

As he had once explained to Karan, so Dulan now carefully explains to Asrafi, 'Karan made a big noise. As a result, Tamadih's Dusadh quarters went up in flames.'

'Where's Karan? Where's Bulaki?'

'Who knows?'

'They're dead.'

'Why do you say that?'

'They've been killed and buried in the jungle.'

'I don't know. But keep the hakim, the village doctor, with you when you act.'

'All right.'

'Get the hakim to help you later, too. That time, they paid the wages. But later, they lit the fire.'

'I'll tell him.'

∽

In every area, every conflict has a characteristic local pattern.

Lachman Singh says, 'I won't pay that much. Just two rupees and tiffin.'

'Give us the wages, hujoor, protector.'

'Should I?' Lachman Singh's eyes are terribly gentle and sympathetic. He says, 'Let me think about it! You do the same.'

'Even a donkey knows that those wages are fair. But you know what? You mentioned the SDO, right? Go tell him, in these parts, Makhan Singh, Daitari Singh, Ramlagan Singh, Hujuri Prasad Mahato, no one is giving these wages. Why should I alone be ruined?'

Asrafi offers a timid but stubborn smile, 'Ruined, hujoor? You own the flour mill, your mansion can be seen from miles away—how can you be ruined?'

To Lachman Singh this smile is arrogant mockery. He says, 'The rate I mentioned is what we decided amongst us. Because we own land, the sarkar treats us like thieves. Yet you get sarkari aid for whatever little land you have. I've given Dulan land. The bastard doesn't farm it, but he collects seeds every year. Animal! He eats them. So let him. And what aid do we get? Fertilizer, seeds, insecticide, we have to buy everything ourselves. Tell the SDO what I said.'

Asrafi tells Dulan, 'Be careful, Chacha! The bastard knows that you don't farm the land or harvest crops.'

The corpses weigh even heavier on Dulan's mind. Lachman Singh has warned him, 'Don't sow or plough the land for a few years, Dulan.'

Dulan, sorrowfully and with deep concern for Asrafi, says,

'Don't trust him, beta. Your father performed the birth rites for my Dhatua-Latua.'

'No, Chacha.'

Asrafi keeps shuttling between the SDO and Lachman Singh. Dulan grows increasingly depressed. Fearing some calamity, he growls at his sons, 'The son of the lowborn will always be lowborn. You eat whatever I manage to wring from the soil. Someone else would have gone off to a nearby colliery. Why are you hanging on here?'

Dhatua raises his calm, dreamy eyes and says, 'This time we'll get double wages, Baba.'

Dulan says nothing further. He goes to the block office at Tohri, says, 'This time I want to sow rabi after the harvest. I need help.'

∽

The BDO seems to know the irrefutable reason for continuing to supply seeds for land that will never be farmed. He, too, joins Lachman and Dulan in this conspiracy and, smiling toothily, says, 'I'll look into it.'

Dulan notices the huge trees in his compound. Such tall papaya trees are rare.

He says, 'How did this papaya tree grow so tall, babu?'

The BDO gives a deeply self-satisfied smile, 'This area became a part of the office compound later. During the summer they would shoot mad dogs and dump them in the hole there. Trees are bound to grow well if they're fertilized by rotting bones and flesh.'

'Does it make good fertilizer?'

'Very good. Haven't you seen how flowers flourish on the burial mounds of poor Muslims?'

These words cause the corpses to weigh lighter in Dulan's mind. Returning to his village, Dulan goes to the land in the middle of the afternoon. Yes, true enough! Karan and Bulaki are now those putush bushes and aloe plants! Tears strain at his eyes. 'Karan, you haven't died even in death. But these putush bushes and aloe plants are of no use to anybody, even buffaloes and goats don't eat them. You fought for our rights. Why couldn't you turn into maize or wheat? Or, at the very least, china grass? So we could eat ghato made of the boiled seeds?'

Sorrowing and bitter, he goes to Tamadih. Nobody is around, so he dismantles the fence protecting Lachman Singh's vegetable patch. He rounds up a few buffaloes and clicks his tongue 'Har, har, har' and drives them into the vegetable patch. Then he goes the long way around to the front of the house and says to Lachman Singh, 'Malik, protector, write me a letter. I want admission into hospital. Cough and chest pain.'

'I'll give you the letter after the harvesting.'

'Very good, master.'

Once more, the corpses weigh Dulan down. He returns to the patch of land, digging into the depths of his mind with the pickaxe of anxiety. Tells Karan and Bulaki to move over and make space.

After the harvesting is over? Is someone coming to keep Karan and Bulaki company?

The harvesting is underway. After much debate, two rupees fifty paise a day and a snack are decided upon. Lachman Singh supervises the harvest on horseback. The police ceremonially make an appearance and confirm that the harvesting is peaceful. On the seventh day, everyone gets their wages.

Heaving a sigh of relief, the SDO leaves with the police.

On the eighth day, the storm breaks. Lachman Singh brings in outside labourers to harvest the paddy. Asrafi and the others feel threatened, and, though scared, they speak up stubbornly.

'You can't do this.'

'Who says so? I am doing it. Sons of bitches, see for yourself—I can do it.'

'But—'

'I let you work. I paid you your wages. Bas—the game's over!'

Seeing Asrafi and the others on the verge of creating trouble, the outsiders lower their scythes and huddle together. Shots are fired. The outside labourers flee.

Shots are fired.

There is no account of the number shot dead. According to Dulan and the others, eleven. According to Lachman Singh and the police, seven. Asrafi's father loses his sons. Two sons, Mohar and Asrafi, both missing. Mahuban Kairi of Chama village and Paras Dhobi of Burudiha—missing. Cries of mourning in almost every home. When the SDO arrives, the fathers, mothers, wives, children of the dead and missing fall at his feet. The SDO's face is as if hewn from rock. He promises the villagers that he'll file a police case against Lachman Singh. He's telling the reporters the whole story, escorting them around. Until the warrant comes, Lachman Singh is not to leave home.

∽

On a moonlit night, when there's a nip in the sweet-scented air, Lachman Singh arrives. Everything in these areas follows a pattern, and the noblest animal is the four-footed horse... Four horses carrying four corpses. This time, Lachman's men help Dulan. Deep, deep pits are needed. The land is soaked with monsoon rain and autumn dew. Four corpses piled one on the other. The burden within Dulan grows even heavier.

Dulan becomes increasingly strange. He picks quarrels at the BD office to extract more and more seeds. Money for a plough and buffalo. Then, before the month is out, a few aloe plants bring solace. Very healthy, very green aloe plants and putush bushes accept the salutations of the sun each dawn during the Emergency in neglected southeast Bihar, silent testimony to the murder of field labourers cum Harijans. Lachman is released without being charged. Emergency. The SDO is demoted for undermining the harmony between the labourers and the landowners by inciting the former to revolt. Lachman and the other jotedars and mahajans offer puja at Hanuman Misra's temple with savage fanfare and a hundred and eight pure-silver bael leaves, and announce that only those sons and daughters of curs and bitches who are willing to work for one rupee without food or water, need bother to show up. They can bring in outside labour.

The Emergency has caused widespread calamity in the region. Congress musclemen have contracted to get outside labourers. Now the game hots up, becomes even more cruelly entertaining. Four annas out of each days' wages have to be given to the contractor. Whether you are contracted by him or not. These musclemen have vowed that they'll get the crop harvested at gunpoint, and anyone who dares object will be doused in petrol and set on fire, so that matters are settled once and for all.

Dulan wanders around with a heavy mind, and looking at Dhatua-Latua, wonders if they should flee. But where can they go? Where will a Dulan Ganju be safe in his motherland of southeast Bihar?

Is there a place without Lachman Singhs?

During the Holi festival, he doesn't even listen to the songs carefully. But suddenly the joyous celebrations are interrupted by a strange song. Dhatua, intoxicated with mahwa, plays the tuila and sings, his eyes closed:

Where has Karan gone?
And Bulaki?
Why is there no news of them?
They are lost in the police files.
Where is Asrafi Hajam?
And his brother Mohar?
Where are Mahuban and Paras?
Why is there no news of them?
They are lost in the police files.
Karan fought the twenty-five-paise battle.

Asrafi fought the five-rupees-forty-paise battle.
Bulaki and Mohar
Fought alongside their elder brothers.
Mahuban could brew the best mahwa
Paras was the best Holi dance
All lost in the police files, lost.

The song ends. Everyone is silent. The colours of Holi turn to ash, the intoxication wears off. Dulan stands up.

'Who made up this song?'

'I did, Baba.'

Dulan broke into deep sobs. He said, 'Forget that song. Or you too will get lost in the police files.'

Dulan returned to his land. Climbed down the embankment, into the middle of the patch. In an eerie whisper he said, 'You've become songs. You hear? Songs. Songs made up by my son Dhatua. You've become gaan, song, not dhaan, paddy, not china grass—now get off my chest, I can't take it any more!'

Under the full Holi moon, the fresh leaves of the aloe plants and the rough-barked putush bushes shook with laughter. They had never heard anything so funny. Dulan's heart was filled with an unnamed fear for Dhatua. As soon as he climbed the machan, he heard Dhatua's song. Now everyone was singing it. But they were not lost in the police files. Dulan would never be able to reveal everything. The power of Lachman Singh.

∽

One day, the Emergency ends.

One day, the Liberation Sun of India gets off the gaddi, her seat of power, to watch the fun, and then, regaining her breath, a little later, begins agitating to regain the gaddi. One day, Lachman Singh's crop ripens, once again.

After two years of drought-famine-crop-destruction, this year the earth generously floods the land with paddy. Paddy fields disappearing into the horizon, punctuated with rows of machans. Birds feed on the ripening paddy day and night.

He who was a Congressman and muscleman and field-labour contractor two years ago now expunges the title 'Congress and muscleman' from his name and appears as the Contractor of Field Labour. With him are a Terylene-and-dark-glasses-flaunting, gun-toting foursome, all exactly like him. In an Amitabh Bachchan voice, this mercenary tells Lachman Singh, 'Your days are over. Now, strike-breaking, supplying contract labour and harvesting is managed by professionals. I provide mercenary services in southeastern Bihar. This service is compulsory. Five thousand bucks. Advance.'

'Five thousand?'

'Are you willing to pay the sarkar's fixed wage rate?'

'No, no.'

'By not paying those rates, you stand to make a profit of eighty thousand. And you don't want to pay five thousand?'

'I'll pay.'

'Bas. Give me the names of the villages and the labourers. Any troublemakers?'

'No.'

'All right. I have to provide services to Ramlagan Singh and Makhan Singh, too. I'll come at the appropriate time. And yes, pay them five sikka as wages. My share is four annas.'

'One rupee.'

'Five sikka. Amarnath Misra doesn't waste words.'

'How are you related to Misraji and Tahar?'

'Bhatija. His brother's son. The seed capital for my services was provided by Chachaji himself.'

Thus everything is settled. Later, Hanuman Misra says to Lachman Singh, 'Yes, yes, he's my bhatija. I bought surface collieries for my sons, and asked him, "Shall I get you one, too?" But no, he didn't want such tiresome work. Very competent and efficient. Election candidates use his services, as do owners of factories on strike. He supplied labour for surface collieries. Very efficient! Three wives. Keeps them in different towns. Built a house for each one. The previous sarkar knew his worth. Not one of my sons turned out as clever as him.'

Lachman Singh, a ruthless Rajput, is all-powerful in his own territory. But even he accepts that this time he has no choice but to accept the services of the mercenaries who are being forced down his throat. If he doesn't, Makhan and Ramlagan will score over him by availing of the services of the gunmen, while his own work will not be done.

Harvesting begins. No outside labourers. Dhatua and the others are doing it themselves. A snack of corn sattu, chilli, salt and five sikka daily wages. Dhatua's mother packs some pickle of wild karamcha for her two sons to go with the snack.

Dulan sits on the machan. Sits and waits—for what? Harvesting is going on. In the distance, the women are singing as they reap. It sounds like a lullaby. But Dulan can't sleep.

Who has stolen the sleep from Dulan's eyes?
His sleep is lost in the police files.

Dulan waits at home for Dhatua and Latua to return. Then he goes to his land. In the monsoons, wet with showers and the autumn dew, the aloe plants and putush bushes stand arrogant, like a rampant jungle. The bushes are bursting with flowers. Sleep eludes Dulan's eyes.

The expected trouble begins on pay day. Amarnath demands his share. Lachman says, 'No bloodshed, please. You and I have no agreement about cutting your share from the wages. Settle it with them.'

'With all of them? Amarnath laughs like a hyena. '*You* pay me.'

Dulan's son, Dhatua, resists the most. That's why Lachman Singh doesn't want to get involved. He knows only one way of dealing with the untouchable and that is a bullet from his gun. This is one person he doesn't want to shoot. Dulan is too useful to him.

Amarnath says, 'Talk to these curs? Five sikka for five hundred people. One sikka per day per head works out to one thousand eight hundred seventy-five rupees for fifteen days. Hand it over.'

'No, hujoor! We won't,' Dhatua protests.

Lachman sighs. Once again, he will have to work according to his usual pattern. Once again he will have to pick up his gun. Karan went, Asrafi came, Asrafi went, now there's Dhatua.

'How can we take home fifteen rupees for fifteen days? Shouldn't we get eighteen rupees twelve annas? Wasn't that agreed upon? We haven't delayed the work, have we?'

'Watch it, Dhatua.'

Lachman Singh hands over the money to Amarnath. Then he says, 'Don't say a word, Dhatua. Just leave.'

Karan was raucous with his demands. Asrafi was aggressive. Dhatua had never known that he could protest so stubbornly over this matter of cutting Amarnath's share from their wages. Stepping out, he tells the others, 'You carry on. I'll settle things before I leave here.'

He returns to face Lachman Singh. Says, 'If you don't settle the account for the remaining twenty-five paise, we won't come to work tomorrow. The best fields are not yet done. We won't work, and we won't let anyone else work, either.'

'You're lucky the police are here for their cut, Dhatua. You're safe this time.'

'Why? Do the police scare you?'

Dhatua leaves, but this last barb enrages Lachman Singh. Even so, since Dhatua is Dulan's son, and Dulan is necessary to his secret, Lachman Singh gives the lower castes a day's time.

The next day, everyone comes, but no one works. Lachman is enraged and frustrated. The mercenaries are not available. They have gone to help Makhan Singh and Ramlagan Singh. Outside labour is not available at short notice. As the light fades into evening, Lachman gives his men the necessary instructions: if threats do the trick, don't open fire. Lachman's men ride their horses through the ripe paddy. Having seen several films on the Chambal dacoit gangs, they too have donned khaki green uniforms. They advance. The other side rises and waits.

'Listen here, you whelps, you sons of bitches!'

'You're the son of a bitch!' someone shouts.

They raise their guns. This side storms into the field at amazing speed. They vanish into the paddy. First, verbal missiles speed back and forth.

Then the inevitable bullets fly. Lots of them. Flocks of birds leave the ripe paddy and take flight. In the field, someone gargles blood deep in his throat. A familiar sound.

Then, sharp scythes and iron choppers slash the horses' hooves, keep slashing. The horses and their riders thunder on. The others steal out and flee. Latua and Param run off towards Tohri.

A long, long, agonizing wait for Dulan. Evening turns to night, and the night is far gone when Latua returns.

'Where is Dhatua?'

'I haven't seen him. Hasn't he returned? I went to the police thana.'

'Where is Dhatua?'

'We fetched the police. They'll come here as well. The same SDO, Baba. He's back. He'll come too.'

'Dhatua!'

Why are the corpses stirring deep within Dulan? For whom are they making place? For whom? Realization hits Dulan. He starts up.

'Where are you going?'

'To the land.'

'The boy is missing, and you...you...are you mad, or are you a ghost?'

'Shut up, woman.'

Dulan walks out, begins to run. Dhatua's song, Dhatua's song.

Where has Karan gone?

And Bulaki?

They are lost in the police files.

Dreamy eyes. A birthmark on his hand. Don't you get lost now, Dhatua, don't you get lost. Oh, you aloe plant, you putush bush, don't you laugh at me tonight.

Dhatua is alive, alive.

Lachman Singh. A man. With bloodied face and eyes. Lachman is hitting him. Kicking him. The man falls to the ground.

Two of them, three horses.

Lachman looks at him.

'Come close,' says Dulan.

'Dhatua?'

'Sorry, Dulan, I forbade them, but still these beasts opened fire.'

Lachman kicks the man again. Curses, 'Trigger-happy tough!'

'Dhatua?'

'Buried.'

'Who buried him?'

'This animal.'

'Him?'

'Yes. But don't open your mouth, Dulan. Or else your wife, son, son's wife, grandson, no one will be spared. Take, I'll give you money, lots of money. Your son called the police. I'll buy them off, of course. But remember that I'm sparing Latua only because he's your son. I haven't fired a single bullet today. I could have felled Dhatua with a single shot. I didn't.'

They go away. Dulan can no longer stand there with seven corpses. He falls onto the embankment. Rolls down into the field, torn by the savage leaves and thorns of the aloe plants, till he comes to a halt.

As usual, the investigation remains incomplete. The SDO intervenes. The trigger-happy tough and Amarnath go to jail.

Dhatua does not return.

Dulan ponders, on and on. Finally, he decides to go mad. Because he starts uprooting the aloe and putush from his land at the first Baisakhi showers.

'Where's he gone? In the middle of the afternoon?' his wife asks.

Latua's wife says, 'Father-in-law took the scythe and the shovel and went to the field.'

'Why didn't you stop him?'

'Me? Talk to him?!'

All grief forgotten, his wife rushes out. She climbs the embankment and yells, 'Here, have you gone mad? Why are you trying to clear that jungle?'

'Go home.'

'What do you mean, go home?'

'Go home.'

In tears, his wife goes to the pahaan. The pahaan goes to him. Says, 'Dhatua will come back, Dulan. Don't go crazy in despair over your son. Come, you'll fall ill in the heat of the sun.'

Dulan says, 'Go home, pahaan. Is my son missing or is yours?'

'Yours.'

'Is this my land or yours?'

'Yours.'

'Well, then? I may be mad or I may not. What's it to you? I'll fix that bastard's land!'

'Then get Latua to help you.'

'No, I'll do it all alone.'

Though he doesn't farm, he has green fingers, the pahaan remembers. The pahaan tells Dulan's wife, 'Come let's go home. Let him do what he wants. You have to go to Tohri.'

Dulan's wife and Latua visit Tohri repeatedly to enquire at the thana about Dhatua.

For a few days, Dulan clears the undergrowth. Prepares the land. Then he takes the seeds from his house, telling his wife, 'These seeds are not for eating. I'll sow them.'

'On that land!'

'Yes.'

Scattering the seeds on the land, he chants, like a mantra, 'I won't let you be just aloe and putush. I'll turn you into paddy, Dhatua. I'll turn you into paddy.'

When the seedlings appear, everyone comes to see them. Lachman, Makhan or Ramlagan's fertilizer-fed seedlings are nothing in comparison. These seedlings are as green as they are healthy.

Fallow land, new seedlings. Everyone says so. Dulan, irritated, drives everyone away. He'll do the ploughing and sowing himself, and savour the fresh green by himself.

The pahaan says, 'Lachman Singh would have died of envy if he'd seen this.'

'Who?'

Dulan is indifferent.

'Lachman Singh.'

'Where is he?'

'Gone to Gaya. To his in-laws' place.'

'Oh!'

Then the paddy grows. Tall, strong, healthy plants. A wonderful crop. The paddy ripens. Now Dulan's extreme insanity is revealed.

He says, 'I'm not going to harvest the crop.'

'What? After all the labour of cutting the canal and draining the stagnant water this past monsoon, after staying there day and night, after I wore myself to death carting ghato and water for you each day—you won't reap?'

'No, and no one is to come here. I've work to do.'

'What work? Just sitting?'

'Yes. Just sitting.'

What he was waiting for occurred. Lachman returned for the harvest. The news of Dulan's bumper crop reached him. A year has passed since Dhatua's murder. Lachman is in control of himself again.

Lachman comes to Dulan. Dulan knew he would come. He knew.

'Dulan.'

'Malik, protector?'

'Come here.'

'What's this, you're alone?'

'Don't talk rubbish. What's the meaning of this?'

'What?'

'Why is there paddy on this land?'

'I planted it.'

'What was agreed between us?'

'You tell me.'

'Son of a bitch, didn't I tell you not to farm this land? To leave it as jungle—'

Dulan below, Lachman on horseback. All at once, Dulan grabbed Lachman's foot and pulled hard. Lachman fell. His rifle flew and landed some distance away from him. Then the rifle was in Dulan's hand. Before Lachman could recover his wits, the butt of the rifle slammed into his head. Lachman screamed. Dulan smashed the butt into his collar bone. A snapping sound.

Son of a bitch, bastard... Frightened, Lachman realized that he was crying before Dulan. Tears of agony and terror. He, Lachman Singh, prostrate on the ground, and Dulan Ganju standing erect? He lunged at Dulan's foot and winced because Dulan had hurled a rock at his outstretched hand. It would be a long time before he could use his right hand again.

'Animal! Cur!'

'What was our agreement, malik? That I shouldn't farm. Why not? You'll sow corpses, and I'll guard them. Why? Otherwise you'll burn down the village, kill my family. Very good. But, malik, seven boys—seven. Is it right for only wild, thorny underbrush to grace their graves? So, I sowed paddy, you see. Everyone says I've gone mad. I have, you know. I won't let you go today, malik, I won't let you harvest your crop. Won't let you shoot, burn houses, kill people. You've harvested enough.'

'Do you think the police will let you go?'

'If they don't, they don't. Your henchmen, too, will probably go for me. But when haven't they, malik? Has the police ever let up on us? So they'll beat me—if I die, so be it. Everyone dies sometime. Did Dhatua die before his time?'

Knowing that he was helpless, Lachman Singh was filled with the fear of death. But even in the throes of this fear, in southeast Bihar, the Rajput will never beg the lowborn for mercy. Even if he did, the lowborn will not always be able to gift him his life. As Dulan could not.

As Lachman tried his best to stand up, shout, or lift a stone with his left hand, Dulan said, 'What a pity, malik! You had to die by a Ganju's hand!'

He began to smash Lachman's head with a rock. Over and over again. Lachman, a professional killer, knew the value of a bullet, so murder was no cause for disturbance. He would have killed Dulan with a single bullet.

Dulan is not used to killing, a rock has no value, this death is the result of years of intense mental turmoil. He continued to smash Lachman's head in till he knew he could stop.

Dulan stood up. There were many things to be done, one by one. He led the horse forward by the reins, brought a stick down on its haunches and drove it off. Let it go where it will. He lashed Lachman, gun and all, with a rope, dragged him away and dumped him in a ditch. Then he rolled stone after stone into it. Stone after stone. Laughter begins to well up inside him. So, malik, protector, you're like the disgusting Oraon Munda? Buried under stones? A stony grave?

No tell-tale signs were likely to remain on the hard, rocky ground. But he broke off a leafy branch from a nearby putush bush to sweep away any marks of a struggle. Then he climbed onto the machan.

The search for Lachman continued for a few days. Since he

never consulted anyone, Lachman had not mentioned that he was going to see Dulan. This was only natural, since his dependence on Dulan had to be kept secret. Those of his henchmen who knew kept their mouths shut. When the malik protector himself goes missing, when his horse is discovered grazing on Daitari Singh's land, why irritate a fresh wound? Lachman's servant said, 'He drank his sweetened milk as usual, and rode off. How do I know where he went?'

A very strange business. Only when the hyenas began to howl did people begin to get suspicious. That too, five days later. For five days, the scavengers, smelling flesh beneath the stones, howled, and with great effort shifted the stones, but managed to devour only the face. The strategic cunning with which the corpse was concealed, plus the presence of the horse in his fields, led to Daitari being suspected. Lachman's son supported this view and, because of an old history of feuds, Daitari was questioned for a few days. Then the police gave up for lack of evidence, though Lachman's son and Daitari continued the old tradition of conflict. At no stage did any suspicion touch Dulan. It was natural not to suspect him. Impossible to imagine Dulan killing Lachman, whatever the circumstances.

∽

On the one hand, Lachman-related investigations continue, on the other, a new, contented Dulan descends from the machan. He speaks to the pahaan, and as a result, all of Kuruda village gathers in the pahaan's courtyard one evening.

Dulan says, 'I've never given anyone anything, ever.'

Everyone is stunned.

'All of you praised my crop. When I didn't harvest it, you said I was mad. While I was farming, you called me mad. You called this fool a fool. Now listen to what this madman has to say.'

'Go ahead!'

There is a sense of relief after Lachman's death. Right now, no one wants to worry about the son taking on the father's role.

'My paddy is your seed. Take it.'

'You're giving it away?'

'Yes, take it, reap it. There's a long story behind this—did I use fertilizer? Yes I did, very precious fertilizer.' Dulan's voice disappears like the string of a severed kite losing itself in the sky. Then, clearing his throat, he says, 'You harvest it. Give me some as well, I'll sow it again and again.'

After they promise that they will harvest the crop when the time came, Dulan returns to his land. His heart is strangely, wonderfully light today! He stands on the embankment and looks at the paddy.

Karan, Asrafi, Mohar, Bulaki, Mahuban, Paras and Dhatua—what amazing joy there is in the ripe, green paddy nourished on your flesh and bones! Because you will be seed. To be a seed is to stay alive. Slowly, Dulan climbs up to the machan. A tune in his heart. Dhatua made up this song. Dhatua, Dulan's voice trembles as he says the name. Dhatua, I've turned you all into seed.

FIVE

~

BEING MORTAL*

ATUL GAWANDE

I am leery of suggesting the idea that endings are controllable. No one ever really has control. Physics and biology and accident ultimately have their way in our lives. But the point is that we are not helpless either. Courage is the strength to recognize both realities. We have room to act, to shape our stories, though as time goes on it is within narrower and narrower confines. A few conclusions become clear when we understand this: that our most cruel failure in how we treat the sick and the aged is the failure to recognize that they have priorities beyond merely being safe and living longer; that the chance to shape one's story is essential to sustaining meaning in life; that we have the opportunity to refashion our institutions, our culture, and our conversations in ways that transform the possibilities for the last chapters of everyone's lives.

*This extract is taken from *Being Mortal: Medicine and What Matters in the End* by Atul Gawande, published by Penguin Books, 2015.

Inevitably, the question arises of how far those possibilities should extend at the very end—whether the logic of sustaining people's autonomy and control requires helping them to accelerate their own demise when they wish to. "Assisted suicide" has become the term of art, though advocates prefer the euphemism "death with dignity." We clearly already recognize some form of this right when we allow people to refuse food or water or medications and treatments, even when the momentum of medicine fights against it. We accelerate a person's demise every time we remove someone from an artificial respirator or artificial feeding. After some resistance, cardiologists now accept that patients have the right to have their doctors turn off their pacemaker—the artificial pacing of their heart—if they want it. We also recognize the necessity of allowing doses of narcotics and sedatives that reduce pain and discomfort even if they may knowingly speed death. All proponents seek is the ability for suffering people to obtain a prescription for the same kind of medications, only this time to let them hasten the timing of their death. We are running up against the difficulty of maintaining a coherent philosophical distinction between giving people the right to stop external or artificial processes that prolong their lives and giving them the right to stop the natural, internal processes that do so.

At root, the debate is about what mistakes we fear most—the mistake of prolonging suffering or the mistake of shortening valued life. We stop the healthy from committing suicide because we recognize that their psychic suffering is often temporary. We believe that, with help, the remembering self will later see matters differently than the experiencing self—and indeed only a minority of people saved from suicide make a repeated attempt; the vast majority eventually report being glad to be alive. But for the terminally ill who face suffering that we know will increase, only the stonehearted can be unsympathetic.

All the same, I fear what happens when we expand the terrain of medical practice to include actively assisting people with speeding their death. I am less worried about abuse of these powers than I am about dependence on them. Proponents have crafted the authority to be tightly circumscribed to avoid error and misuse. In places that allow physicians to write lethal prescriptions—countries like the Netherlands, Belgium, and Switzerland and states like Oregon, Washington, and Vermont—they can do so only for terminally ill adults who face unbearable suffering, who make repeated requests on separate occasions, who are certified not to be acting out of depression or other mental illness, and who have a second physician confirming they meet the criteria. Nonetheless, the larger culture invariably determines how such authority is employed. In the Netherlands, for instance, the system has existed for decades, faced no serious opposition, and significantly grown in use. But the fact that, by 2012, one in thirty-five Dutch people sought assisted suicide at their death is not a measure of success. It is a measure of failure. Our ultimate goal, after all, is not a good death but a good life to the very end. The Dutch have been slower than others to develop palliative care programs that might provide for it. One reason, perhaps, is that their system of assisted death may have reinforced beliefs that reducing suffering and improving lives through other means is not feasible when one becomes debilitated or seriously ill.

Certainly, suffering at the end of life is sometimes unavoidable and unbearable, and helping people end their misery may be necessary. Given the opportunity, I would support laws to provide these kinds of prescriptions to people. About half don't even use their prescription. They are reassured just to know they have this control if they need it. But we damage entire societies if we let providing this capability divert us from improving the lives of the ill. Assisted living is far harder than assisted death, but its possibilities are far greater, as well.

In the throes of suffering, this can be difficult to see. One day I got a call from the husband of Peg Bachelder, my daughter Hunter's piano teacher. "Peg's in the hospital," Martin said.

I'd known she had serious health issues. Two and a half years earlier, she'd developed a right hip pain. The condition was misdiagnosed for almost a year as arthritis. When it got worse, one physician even recommended seeing a psychiatrist and gave her a book on "how to let go of your pain." But imaging finally revealed that she had a five-inch sarcoma, a rare soft-tissue cancer, eating into her pelvis and causing a large blood clot in her leg. Treatment involved chemotherapy, radiation, and radical surgery removing a third of her pelvis and reconstructing it with metal. It was a year in hell. She was hospitalized for months with complications. She'd loved cycling, yoga, walking her Shetland sheepdog with her husband, playing music, and teaching her beloved students. She'd had to let go of all of that.

Eventually, however, Peg recovered and was able to return to teaching. She needed Canadian crutches—the kind that have a cuff around the forearm—to get around but otherwise remained her graceful self and refilled her roster of students in no time. She was sixty-two, tall, with big round glasses, a thick bob of auburn hair, and a lovely gentle way that made her an immensely popular teacher. When my daughter struggled with grasping a sound or technique, Peg was never hurried. She'd have her try this and then try that, and when Hunter finally got it, Peg would burble with genuine delight and hug her close.

A year and a half after returning, Peg was found to have a leukemia-like malignancy caused by her radiation treatment. She went back on chemotherapy but somehow kept teaching through it. Every few weeks, she'd have to reschedule Hunter's lesson, and we had to explain the situation to Hunter, who was just thirteen at the time. But Peg always found a way to keep going.

Then for two straight weeks, she postponed the lessons. That was when I got the call from Martin. He was phoning from the hospital. Peg had been admitted for several days. He put his cell on speaker so she could talk. She sounded weak—there were long pauses when she spoke—but she was clear-voiced about the situation. The leukemia treatment had stopped working a few weeks before, she said. She developed a fever and infection due to her compromised immune system. Imaging also showed her original cancer had come back in her hip and in her liver. The recurrent disease began to cause immobilizing hip pain. When it made her incontinent, that felt like the final straw. She checked into the hospital at that point, and she didn't know what to do.

What had the doctors told her they could do? I asked.

"Not much," she said. She sounded flat, utterly hopeless. They were giving her blood transfusions, pain medications, and steroids for tumor-caused fevers. They'd stopped giving her chemotherapy.

I asked her what her understanding of her condition was.

She said she knew she was going to die. There's nothing more they can do, she said, an edge of anger creeping into her voice.

I asked her what her goals were, and she didn't have any she could see possible. When I asked what her fears for the future were, she named a litany: facing more pain, suffering the humiliation of losing more of her bodily control, being unable to leave the hospital. She choked up as she spoke. She'd been there for days just getting worse, and she feared she didn't have many more. I asked her if they'd talked to her about hospice. They had, she said, but she didn't see what it could do to help her.

Some in her position, offered "death with dignity," might have taken it as the only chance for control when no other options seemed apparent. Martin and I persuaded Peg to try hospice. It'd at least let her get home, I said, and might help her more than she knew. I explained how hospice's aim, at least in theory, was to give people their best possible day, however they might define it under the circumstances. It seemed like it had been a while since she'd had a good day, I said.

"Yes, it has—a long while," she said.

That seemed worth hoping for, I said—just one good day.

She went home on hospice within forty-eight hours. We broke the news to Hunter that Peg would not be able to give her lessons anymore, that she was dying. Hunter was struck low. She adored Peg. She wanted to know if she could see her one more time. We had to tell her that we didn't think so.

A few days later, we got a surprising call. It was Peg. If Hunter was willing, she said, she'd like to resume teaching her. She'd understand if Hunter didn't want to come. She didn't know how many more lessons she could manage, but she wanted to try.

That hospice could make it possible for her to teach again was more than I'd ever imagined, certainly more than she'd imagined. But when her hospice nurse, Deborah, arrived, they began talking about what Peg cared most about in her life, what having the best day possible would really mean to her. Then they worked together to make it happen.

At first, her goal was just managing her daily difficulties. The hospice team set up a hospital bed on the first floor so she wouldn't have to navigate the stairs. They put a portable commode at the bedside. They organized help for bathing and getting dressed. They gave her morphine, gabapentin, and oxycodone to control her pain, and methylphenidate proved helpful for combating the stupor they induced.

Her anxieties plummeted as the challenges came under control. She raised her sights. "She was focused on the main chance," Martin later said. "She came to a clear view of how she wanted to live the rest of her days. She was going to be home, and she was going to teach."

It took planning and great expertise to make each lesson possible. Deborah helped her learn how to calibrate her medications. "Before she would teach, she would take some additional morphine. The trick was to give her enough to be comfortable to teach and not so much that she would be groggy," Martin recalled.

Nonetheless, he said, "She was more alive running up to a lesson and for the days after." She'd had no children; her students filled that place for her. And she still had some things she wanted them to know before she went. "It was important to her to be able to say her goodbyes to her dear friends, to give her parting advice to her students."

She lived six full weeks after going on hospice. Hunter had lessons for four of them, and then two final concerts were played. One featured Peg's former students, accomplished performers from around the country, the other her current students, all children in middle school and high school. Gathered together in her living room, they played Brahms, Dvořák, Chopin, and Beethoven for their adored teacher.

Technological society has forgotten what scholars call the "dying role" and its importance to people as life approaches its end. People want to share memories, pass on wisdoms and keepsakes, settle relationships, establish their legacies, make peace with God, and ensure that those who are left behind will be okay. They want to end their stories on their own terms. This role is, observers argue, among life's most important, for both the dying and those left behind. And if it is, the way we deny people this role, out of obtuseness and neglect, is cause for everlasting shame. Over and over, we in medicine inflict deep gouges at the end of people's lives and then stand oblivious to the harm done.

Peg got to fulfill her dying role. She got to do so right up to three days before the end, when she fell into delirium and passed in and out of consciousness.

My final remembrance of her is from near the end of her last recital. She'd taken Hunter away from the crowd and given her a book of music she wanted her to keep. Then she put her arm around her shoulder.

"You're special," she whispered to her. It was something she never wanted Hunter to forget.

SIX

~

THE SHROUD*

MUNSHI PREMCHAND

Translated from the Urdu by Muhammad Umar Memon

Outside the hut, father and son sat in silence in front of the fire pit already gone cold. Inside, Budhya, the son's young wife, kept thrashing about in labour, intermittently sending forth piercing cries of pain that momentarily froze the hearts of the two men. It was a cold, wintry night. Stillness pervaded all around. The entire village was engulfed in darkness.

'Doesn't look like she'll make it,' said Ghisu. 'She's been writhing in agony all day long. Perhaps you should go in and have a look at her.'

Madhu replied in a mournful voice, 'If die she must, why linger on. What's there for me to look at, anyway?'

'You are a heartless man... So unfeeling towards the woman who gave you every comfort of life for an entire year!'

*This story is taken from *The Greatest Urdu Stories Ever Told* edited by Muhammad Umar Memon, published by Aleph Book Company, 2017.

'I just can't bear the sight of her flailing about in utter agony.'

Theirs was a family of chamars, and none too liked for its ways throughout the village. Ghisu worked one day and took rest for the next three. Madhu shirked work if he could help it. And even if he did work for an hour, he spent an equal amount smoking his chillum. That's why no one felt like hiring these layabouts. If the house had a fistful of grain, well, that was as good a reason as any not to work at all. When, however, they had to go without food for a couple of times, Ghisu climbed on trees and broke some branches, which Madhu then took to the bazaar to sell. For the time the money lasted, the two idled away without a care, until the next bout of starvation overtook them, and the earlier routine of gathering firewood or looking for work kicked in again. It wasn't like there was shortage of work in this village of farmers. Hundreds of jobs were ready for the taking for any hardworking man. People took them on only when necessity drove them to hire two men to do the job of one. Had the two been only sadhus, there would be absolutely no need to seek contentment and trust in God through ascetic self-denial, for these were their innate attributes. It was a strange life; they owned nothing beyond a few clay pots, torn rags to clothe their nakedness—free of worldly deceptions, weighed down by heavy debts, the butt of people's insults and scorn, and yet not a worry to speak of. Despite their abject poverty, people still lent them something, fully aware that none of it was ever coming back. At harvest time, they would steal green peas or dig up potatoes from other people's fields, bake them and have their fill, or pick a few stalks of sugarcane to suck at night. Ghisu had lived through all his sixty years in such ascetic frugality, and Madhu, every bit his father's son, was following in his footsteps; if anything, he had put a gloss on his old man's fame. Ghisu's wife had died a while back. Madhu had married just a year ago. Ever since her arrival, this woman had put a measure of order and civility in their family. She would do chores for others; grind grain or cut grass to earn a little and buy some flour to fill the stomachs of these shameless bums. Her presence had made them even more indolent and slothful. If anyone offered a job, they audaciously asked for double wages, as if they couldn't care less. And now the same woman was writhing in deathly labour since the morning, while the two men were perhaps waiting for her to kick the bucket so that they could finally get some peaceful sleep.

Ghisu yanked out the potatoes from the ashes, started peeling them, and told Madhu, 'Come on now, go inside and see how she's doing. Looks like some evil spirit has possessed her—yes, evil spirit, a witch. Here, even an exorcist asks for a rupee. Who's going to give it to us?'

Afraid that if he went inside Ghisu would polish off most of the potatoes himself, Madhu said, 'I'm scared.'

'Scared—scared of what? I'm right here.'

'Well then, go yourself and see.'

'When my woman lay dying, I didn't leave her side for three days. Wouldn't Budhya be embarrassed seeing me? I've never seen her face without her veil on. If she sees me in her senseless state, she wouldn't be able to thrash freely out of modesty.'

'Say, what if she did give birth to a child? Ginger, raw sugar, oil—we have got nothing in the house.'

'Oh, we'll get everything. First, let Bhagwan give us a child. The very people who are averse to giving us a paisa now will rush in to provide. Nine boys were born to us and we were flat broke, but each time things worked out swimmingly.'

The emergence of such a mindset was not surprising, indeed it was inevitable in a social milieu where the general condition of those toiling away day and night was not much better than that of Ghisu and Madhu and where carefree existence was the privilege of only those who took advantage of the dismal circumstances of the peasantry. One would even venture to say that Ghisu reflected a keener sense of reality and discernment than the peasants in joining the ranks of the rogues and the rabble-rousers rather than those of the dim-witted community of farm workers. What he sorely lacked, though, was the ability to stick to rules and ways of the rogues. So, while others of his ilk became wielders of power and authority in the village, he remained the object of everyone's scorn. But there was comfort in the thought that as bad as his situation was at least he didn't have to work his backside off like farmers, that his simple-mindedness and unassuming manner were his greatest assets against anyone taking advantage of him.

Both men pulled out searing hot potatoes and started eating ravenously. They hadn't had a morsel to eat since the day before and could hardly wait for the potatoes to cool. As a result, they repeatedly singed their tongues. The outer part of a peeled potato didn't feel overly hot, but the instant the teeth dug into its inside, the burning pulp scalded their tongues, their palates, and their throats. It was better to quickly swallow the live ember than chew on it. It would be cooled once it had plopped into their stomachs anyway. They hurriedly swallowed the embers; however, the effort caused their eyes to water profusely.

As they gobbled the potatoes, Ghisu remembered the day when, twenty years ago, he was part of the Thakur's wedding procession. He had eaten so much and so well at the banquet that day that it became the most memorable event of his life. Its memory was still vividly alive in his mind. He said, 'Would I ever forget that fabulous meal! I haven't had anything quite like it ever since. It was out of this world. I could eat as much as I wanted. The bride's family served fried puris. Bigshots and nobodys, all—and I mean all—ate puris and satpanis made from pure ghee, raita, three types of dried-leaf vegetable dishes, another kind of vegetable dish, dahi, chutney, and sweetmeats! I cannot begin to tell you how fantastic the food tasted. You could eat as much as you wanted, ask for anything, and eat until you could no more. People ate so much, so much they had no room left for a drink of water. But those serving the food kept piling up our plates with piping hot and perfectly round fragrant kachoris, regardless of how much we asked them not to or shielded our plates with hands. They just didn't know how to stop. When the guests had rinsed their mouths and washed their hands, they were each offered a cone of paan. But I had no mind to chew paan. I could hardly stand up. I made it to my blanket and splayed out on it as fast as I could. Such was the generosity of the Thakur! It knew no bounds!'

Madhu, savouring these flavourful delicacies in his imagination, exclaimed, 'If only someone served us such a meal now!'

'Who will? Not a chance. That was a different time. Now people tend to be tight-fisted. They say, "Don't spend too much on weddings! Don't spend too much on funerals!" Just ask them, "So what are you going to do with what all you have been squeezing out of the poor?" Squeezing never stops, frugality kicks in only when it comes to spending.'

'You must have eaten twenty puris, I guess?'

'More than twenty.'

'I would have gobbled fifty.'

'I wouldn't have eaten less than fifty. I was a strapping youth back then. You are not even half as strong.'

After eating the potatoes, they drank some water, covered themselves with their dhotis, and dozed off near the fire pit, curling their legs in foetal position, like two enormous coiled snakes. Meanwhile, Budhya kept groaning in labour.

Come morning, Madhu went inside the hut and found that his wife's body had turned cold. Flies were buzzing around her mouth. Her stony eyes were turned upward in a frozen stare and her body was smeared with dirt and grime. The child had died in her womb.

He rushed out to Ghisu. Both men broke out into loud wailing and started beating their chests. The neighbours came running when they heard their doleful cries. According to the age-old custom, they expressed their sympathy and tried to console them.

However, there wasn't time for much wailing and chest-beating. They had to worry about a shroud for the dead body and wood for the pyre. The money in the house had disappeared like carrion in a buzzard's nest.

Father and son went wailing and crying to the village landlords, who hated the very sight of the two and often had occasion to beat them up for pilfering, for not showing up for work despite promising to. Anyway, they asked, 'What is the matter, Ghisu? Why are you crying? You've become so scarce these days. You aren't thinking of leaving the village, are you?'

Ghisu put down his forehead on the ground and, with tears in his eyes, said, 'Sarkar, a terrible calamity has struck me. Madhu's wife passed away last night. She kept writhing in pain all day long. Both of us stayed by her side half the night. Medicine, drugs, you name it—we tried everything, but she left us all the same. Who would feed us now? Master, we are ruined. The house is desolate. I am your slave. There is only you to help with her cremation. Whatever little we had was spent on medicine and drugs. Her funeral rites will be performed only through your benevolence. At whose door should I go begging if not yours?'

Zamindar Sahib was a gentle soul, but showing mercy to Ghisu was like trying to dye a jet-black fabric a varied colour. He felt like telling him off: 'Get the hell out of here! Keep the corpse in the house and let it rot! When I call you for work, you put on airs and don't show up. Today, when you're in need, you come flattering me—you freeloading son of a bitch! Rascal!'

But this was hardly the time to get angry or seek revenge. Zamindar Sahib took out two rupees and disdainfully threw them at him, without a word of commiseration. He didn't bother to even look at him, as if he just wanted to get this weight off his chest, and get it off pretty damn quick.

Once the Zamindar had dished out two rupees, how dare the banias and moneylenders of the village refuse him? He went around announcing loudly that the Zamindar had donated two rupees. People gave, some two annas, some four. Within an hour Ghisu had bagged a tidy sum of five rupees. Some offered grain, some others wood. Around noon both men set out for the bazaar to buy a shroud, and others started to chop bamboo stalks to fashion a bier for the corpse.

The tender-hearted womenfolk of the village came to look at Budhya's dead body, shed a few tears at the hapless woman and left.

~

After they had made it to the bazaar, Ghisu said, 'We've got enough wood for the pyre, Madhu, what do you say?'

'Oh yes, plenty,' Madhu replied. 'All we need now is the shroud.'

'Well then, let's get a cheap one.'

'Of course, a cheap one. By the time the corpse is carried off for cremation, it will be night. No one would care to look at the shroud in the dark.'

'What a lousy custom! Someone who could not get a tattered rag to cover her body while living must have a new shroud now when she dies.'

'A shroud burns up with the corpse.'

'What else! If we had the same five rupees earlier, we could have spent the money on her treatment.'

Both understood the implied meaning of the other. They meandered through the bazaar until evening shadows began to deepen. Whether by accident or by design they found themselves standing right across from a tavern. They walked in, as though driven by some tacit agreement, and stood there hesitating for a bit. Then Ghisu bought a bottle of country liquor and some flats of gajak to go with the drink. They sat on the veranda and began drinking.

A few glasses down their throats in quick succession and both men's heads began to swim.

'What good is a shroud for? It would have burnt to ashes anyway. Bahu wouldn't have carried it with her.'

Madhu looked at the sky, as if trying to prove his innocence to the angels, and said, 'Such are the ways of the world. Why do these moneybags give away thousands of rupees to the Brahmins? Who can tell whether they would get any recompense for it in the next world.'

'The bigshots have plenty to burn, so let them. What have we got to burn?'

'But what will we say to the people? Wouldn't they ask, "Where is the shroud?"'

Ghisu cackled. 'We'll say the money slipped off our waists. We looked and looked but couldn't find it.'

Madhu cackled too. At this unexpected good fortune, and on outsmarting fate, he said, 'Poor woman, she was so good to us. Even in death she's made sure that we are well fed.'

By now they had been through more than half the bottle. Ghisu sent Madhu for two sers of puris, a dish of curried meat, spicy roasted liver, and fried fish. The shop was straight across from the tavern. Madhu returned in no time at all, bringing everything on two leaf platters. It cost them one rupee and a half. They were left with a little bit of change now.

They sat eating with the majestic air of a tiger feasting on his prey, without a care about having to answer for their actions, or haunted by any thought of the coming disgrace. They had overcome such scruples a long time ago. Ghisu said philosophically, 'If our souls are content, wouldn't she get some reward for it!'

Madhu bowed his head with overabundant reverence and agreed, 'Of course she will, no doubt about it. Bhagwan, You are all-knowing! Give her a place in heaven. We pray for her with all our hearts. Never in our life did we taste such delicious food as we did today.'

A split second later Madhu was assailed by doubt. 'Well, Dada, we too will have to go there some day.'

Ghisu brushed aside this childish question and looked at Madhu reproachfully.

'What if she asks us up there, "Why did you people not give my body a shroud?" What will you say?'

'Pipe down.'

'But she will be sure to ask us.'

'How do you know that she won't get her shroud? You think I'm an arsehole or something? I haven't been dawdling all my sixty years. She will get her shroud all right, and she will get a very nice one, much better than what we could have ever given her.'

Madhu, who didn't believe him, said, 'Who is going to give it? You've blown up all the money.'

'I said that she will get a shroud,' Ghisu said in a huff. 'Why don't you believe me?'

'But why won't you tell me who'll give it?'

'The same people who gave this time, except the money won't come into our hands. And if somehow it did, we will again be sitting here drinking away. And we will get a shroud for the third time.'

As the darkness spread and the stars began to shine brightly, the tavern took on an air of exuberance. People broke into song, made merry, hugged their companions, raised wine cups to their friends' lips. The atmosphere was shot through with inebriated gaiety, the air gently intoxicating. It took just a few sips for many to get drunk. People came here for a taste of forgetfulness. Their enjoyment came more from the tavern's ambience than from liquor. Worldly cares had dragged them here—a place where they could forget for a while whether they were alive or dead, or living-dead.

And here they were, father and son, sipping their drinks with a feeling of immense light-heartedness. Everyone's gaze was glued on them: lucky guys, an entire bottle to share between them!

After they were done eating, Madhu picked up the platter of the leftover puris and gave it to the beggar who had been standing nearby, casting greedy looks at them. For the first time in his life Madhu felt the swagger, the elation, the joy that comes from giving.

'Here…take it. Eat your fill,' said Ghisu. 'Give your blessings. The woman who earned this is no more, but your blessings will certainly reach her. Let every pore of your body bless her. It was hard-earned money.'

Madhu looked at the sky again and said, 'Dada, she will surely go to heaven, won't she? She'll become the Queen of Heaven.'

Ghisu stood up and, as if awash in the tide of happiness, said, 'Yes son, she *will*. She will go to heaven. She troubled no one, harmed no one, and even as she lay dying fulfilled the most ardent wish of our life. If she doesn't go to heaven, then will these moneybags who rob the poor folk with both hands and make offerings of holy water at temples and take a dip in the Ganga to wash out their sins?'

The aura of joyful trust in Providence brought on by their inebriated state soon gave way to a bout of despair and sorrow.

'But Dada,' Madhu said, 'she suffered a lot in her life, and not least even when she lay dying.' He covered his eyes with his hands and broke into sobs.

Ghisu tried to comfort him. 'Son, why do you cry? Be glad instead. At least she is rid of the web of earthly illusions, free of worldly cares and anxieties. She was lucky to break free of the bonds of moh and maya so soon.'

Both stood up and started singing at the spot:

Enchantress, why do you entice us with your flashing eyes,
Enchantress!

The entire tavern watched the two tipplers in breathless amazement, who were singing away with abandon, oblivious of everything. Then they started dancing. They skipped and hopped. They stumbled and fell. Swayed their hips seductively. At last, overcome by the stupor brought on by alcohol, they crumbled.

SEVEN

~

THE PORTRAIT OF A LADY*

KHUSHWANT SINGH

My grandmother, like everybody's grandmother, was an old woman. She had been old and wrinkled for the twenty years that I had known her. People said that she had once been young and pretty and had even had a husband, but that was hard to believe. My grandfather's portrait hung above the mantelpiece in the drawing room. He wore a big turban and loose-fitting clothes. His long white beard covered the best part of his chest and he looked at least a hundred years old. He did not look the sort of person who would have a wife or children. He looked as if he could only have lots and lots of grandchildren. As for my grandmother being young and pretty, the thought was almost revolting. She often told us of the games she used to play as a child. That seemed quite absurd and undignified on her part and we treated

*This extract is taken from *Unforgettable Khushwant Singh: His Finest Fiction, Non-Fiction, Poetry and Humour*, published by Aleph Book Company, 2017.

them like the fables of the prophets she used to tell us.

She had always been short and fat and slightly bent. Her face was a criss-cross of wrinkles running from everywhere to everywhere. No, we were certain she had always been as we had known her. Old, so terribly old that she could not have grown older, and had stayed at the same age for twenty years. She could never have been pretty; but she was always beautiful. She hobbled about the house in spotless white, with one hand resting on her waist to balance her stoop and the other telling the beads of her rosary. Her silver locks were scattered untidily over her pale, puckered face, and her lips constantly moved in inaudible prayer. Yes, she was beautiful. She was like the winter landscape in the mountains, an expanse of pure white serenity breathing peace and contentment.

My grandmother and I were good friends. My parents left me with her when they went to live in the city and we were constantly together. She used to wake me up in the morning and get me ready for school. She said her morning prayer in a monotonous sing-song while she bathed and dressed me in the hope that I would listen and get to know it by heart. I listened because I loved her voice but never bothered to learn it. Then she would fetch my wooden slate which she had already washed and plastered with yellow chalk, a tiny earthen inkwpot and a reed pen, tie them all in a bundle and hand it to me. After a breakfast of a thick, stale chapati with a little butter and sugar spread on it, we went to school. She carried several stale chapatis with her for the village dogs.

My grandmother always went to school with me because the school was attached to the temple. The priest taught us the alphabet and the morning prayer. While the children sat in rows on either side of the verandah singing the alphabet or the prayer in a chorus, my grandmother sat inside reading the scriptures. When we had both finished, we would walk back together. This time the village dogs would meet us at the temple door. They followed us to our home growling and fighting each other for the chapatis we threw to them.

When my parents were comfortably settled in the city, they sent for us. That was a turning point in our friendship. Although we shared the same room, my grandmother no longer came to school with me. I used to go to an English school in a motor bus. There were no dogs in the streets and she took to feeding sparrows in the courtyard of our city house.

As the years rolled by we saw less of each other. For some time she continued to wake me up and get me ready for school. When I came back she would ask me what the teacher had taught me. I would tell her English words and little things of Western science and learning, the law of gravity, Archimedes' principle, the world being round, etc. This made her unhappy. She could not help me with my lessons. She did not believe in the things they taught at the English school and was distressed that there was no teaching about God and the scriptures. One day I announced that we were being given music lessons. She was very disturbed. To her music had lewd associations. It was the monopoly of harlots and beggars and not meant for gentlefolk. She rarely talked to me after that.

When I went up to university, I was given a room of my own. The common link of friendship was snapped. My grandmother accepted her seclusion with resignation. She rarely left her spinning wheel to talk to anyone. From sunrise to sunset she sat by her wheel, spinning and reciting prayers. Only in the afternoon she relaxed for a while to feed the sparrows. While she sat in the verandah breaking the bread into little bits, hundreds of little birds collected around her, creating a veritable bedlam of chirrupings. Some came and perched on her legs, others on her shoulders. Some even sat on her head. She smiled but never shooed them away. It used to be the happiest half-hour of the day for her.

When I decided to go abroad for further studies, I was sure my grandmother would be upset. I would be away for five years, and at her age one could never tell. But my grandmother could. She was not even sentimental. She came to leave me at the railway station but did not talk or show any emotion. Her lips moved in prayer, her mind was lost in prayer. Her fingers were busy telling the beads of her rosary. Silently she kissed my forehead, and when I left I cherished the moist imprint as perhaps the last sign of physical contact between us.

But that was not so. After five years I came back home and was met by her at the station. She did not look a day older. She still had no time for words, and while she clasped me in her arms I could hear her reciting her prayer. Even on the first day of my arrival, her happiest moments were with her sparrows, whom she fed longer and with frivolous rebukes.

In the evening a change came over her. She did not pray. She collected the women of the neighbourhood, got an old drum and started to sing. For several hours she thumped the sagging skins of the dilapidated drum and sang of the homecoming of warriors. We had to persuade her to stop to avoid overstraining. That was the first time since I had known her that she did not pray.

The next morning she was taken ill. It was a mild fever and the doctor told us that it would go. But my grandmother thought differently. She told us that her end was near. She said that, since only a few hours before the close of the last chapter of her life she had omitted to pray, she was not going to waste any more time talking to us.

We protested. But she ignored our protests. She lay peacefully in bed, praying and telling her beads. Even before we could suspect, her lips stopped moving and the rosary fell from her lifeless fingers. A peaceful pallor spread on her face and we knew that she was dead.

We lifted her off the bed and, as is customary, laid her on the ground and covered her with a red shroud. After a few hours of mourning we left her alone to make arrangements for her funeral. In the evening we went to her room with a crude stretcher to take her to be cremated. The sun was setting and had lit her room and verandah with a blaze of golden light. We stopped halfway in the courtyard. All over the verandah and in her room right up to where she lay dead and stiff, wrapped in the red shroud, thousands of sparrows sat scattered on the floor. There was no chirping. We felt sorry for the birds and my mother fetched some bread for them. She broke it into little crumbs, the way my grandmother used to, and threw it to them. The sparrows took no notice of the bread. When we carried my grandmother's corpse off, they flew away quietly. Next morning the sweeper swept the bread crumbs into the dustbin.

EIGHT

~

SHOOTING AN ELEPHANT*

GEORGE ORWELL

In Moulmein, in Lower Burma, I was hated by large numbers of people—the only time in my life that I have been important enough for this to happen to me. I was sub-divisional police officer of the town, and in an aimless, petty kind of way anti-European feeling was very bitter. No one had the guts to raise a riot, but if a European woman went through the bazaars alone somebody would probably spit betel juice over her dress. As a police officer I was an obvious target and was baited whenever it seemed safe to do so. When a nimble Burman tripped me up on the football field and the referee (another Burman) looked the other way, the crowd yelled with hideous laughter. This happened more than once. In the end the sneering yellow faces of young men that met me everywhere, the insults hooted after me when I was at a safe distance, got badly on my

*This extract was first published in *New Writing*, 2, Autumn 1936.

nerves. The young Buddhist priests were the worst of all. There were several thousands of them in the town and none of them seemed to have anything to do except stand on street corners and jeer at Europeans.

All this was perplexing and upsetting. For at that time I had already made up my mind that imperialism was an evil thing and the sooner I chucked up my job and got out of it the better. Theoretically—and secretly, of course—I was all for the Burmese and all against their oppressors, the British. As for the job I was doing, I hated it more bitterly than I can perhaps make clear. In a job like that you see the dirty work of Empire at close quarters. The wretched prisoners huddling in the stinking cages of the lock-ups, the grey, cowed faces of the long-term convicts, the scarred buttocks of the men who had been flogged with bamboos—all these oppressed me with an intolerable sense of guilt. But I could get nothing into perspective. I was young and ill-educated and I had had to think out my problems in the utter silence that is imposed on every Englishman in the East. I did not even know that the British Empire is dying, still less did I know that it is a great deal better than the younger empires that are going to supplant it. All I knew was that I was stuck between my hatred of the Empire I served and my rage against the evil-spirited little beasts who tried to make my job impossible. With one part of my mind I thought of the British Raj as an unbreakable tyranny, as something clamped down, *in saecula saeculorum*, upon the will of prostrate peoples; with another part I thought that the greatest joy in the world would be to drive a bayonet into a Buddhist priest's guts. Feelings like these are the normal by-products of imperialism; ask any Anglo-Indian official, if you can catch him off duty.

One day something happened which in a roundabout way was enlightening. It was a tiny incident in itself, but it gave me a better glimpse than I had had before of the real nature of imperialism—the real motives for which despotic governments act. Early one morning the sub-inspector at a police station the other end of town rang me up on the phone and said that an elephant was ravaging the bazaar. Would I please come and do something about it? I did not know what I could do, but I wanted to see what was happening and I got on to a pony and started out. I took my rifle, an old .44 Winchester and much too small to kill an elephant, but I thought the noise might be useful *in terrorem*. Various Burmans stopped me on the way and told me about the elephant's doings. It was not, of course, a wild elephant, but a tame one which had gone 'must'. It had been chained up, as tame elephants always are when their attack of 'must' is due, but on the previous night it had broken its chain and escaped. Its mahout, the only person who could manage it when it was in that state, had set out in pursuit, but had taken the wrong direction and was now twelve hours' journey away, and in the morning the elephant had suddenly reappeared in the town. The Burmese population had no weapons and were quite helpless against it. It had already destroyed somebody's bamboo hut, killed a cow and raided some fruit stalls and devoured the stock; also it had met the municipal rubbish van and, when the driver jumped out and took to his heels, had turned the van over and inflicted violence upon it.

The Burmese sub-inspector and some Indian constables were waiting for me in the quarter where the elephant had been seen. It was a very poor quarter, a labyrinth of squalid bamboo huts, thatched with palm leaf, winding all over a steep hillside. I remember that it was a cloudy, stuffy morning at the beginning of the rains. We began questioning the people as to where the elephant had gone and, as usual, failed to get any definite information. That is invariably the case in the East; a story always sounds clear enough at a distance, but the nearer you get to the scene of events the vaguer it becomes. Some of the people said that the elephant had gone in one direction, some said that he had gone in another, some professed not even to have heard of any elephant. I had almost made up my mind that the whole story was a pack of lies, when we heard yells a little distance away. There was a loud, scandalized cry of 'Go away, child! Go away this instant!' and an old woman with a switch in her hand came round the corner of a hut, violently shooing away a crowd of naked children. Some more women followed, clicking their tongues and exclaiming; evidently there was something that the children ought not to have seen. I rounded the hut and saw a man's dead body sprawling in the mud. He was an Indian, a black Dravidian coolie, almost naked, and he could not have been dead many minutes. The people said that the elephant had come suddenly upon him round the corner of the hut, caught him with its trunk, put its foot on his back and ground him into the earth. This was the rainy season and the ground was soft, and his face had scored a trench a foot deep and a couple of yards long. He was lying on his belly with arms crucified and head sharply twisted to one side. His face was coated with mud, the eyes wide open, the teeth bared and grinning with an expression of unendurable agony. (Never tell me, by the way, that the dead look peaceful. Most of the corpses I have seen looked devilish.) The friction of the great beast's foot had stripped the skin from his back as neatly as one skins a rabbit. As soon as I saw the dead man I sent an orderly to a friend's house nearby to borrow an elephant rifle. I had already sent back the pony, not wanting it to go mad with fright and throw me if it smelt the elephant.

The orderly came back in a few minutes with a rifle and five cartridges, and meanwhile some Burmans had arrived and told us that the elephant was in the paddy fields below, only a few hundred yards away. As I started forward practically the whole population of the quarter flocked out of the houses and followed me. They had seen the rifle and were all shouting excitedly that I was going to shoot the elephant. They had not shown much interest in the elephant when he was merely ravaging their homes, but it was different now that he was going to be shot. It was a bit of fun to them, as it would be to an English crowd; besides they wanted the meat. It made me vaguely uneasy. I had no intention of shooting the elephant—I had merely sent for the rifle to defend myself if necessary—and it is always unnerving to have a crowd following you. I marched down the hill, looking and feeling a fool, with the rifle over my shoulder and an ever-growing army of people jostling at my heels. At the bottom, when you got away from the huts, there was a metalled road and beyond that a miry waste of paddy fields a thousand yards across, not yet ploughed but soggy from the first rains and dotted with coarse grass. The elephant was standing eight yards from the road, his left side towards us. He took not the slightest notice of the crowd's approach. He was tearing up bunches of grass, beating them against his knees to clean them and stuffing them into his mouth.

I had halted on the road. As soon as I saw the elephant I knew with perfect certainty that I ought not to shoot him. It is a serious matter to shoot a working elephant—it is comparable to destroying a huge and costly piece of machinery—and obviously one ought not to do it if it can possibly be avoided. And at that distance, peacefully eating, the elephant looked no more dangerous than a cow. I thought then and I think now that his attack of 'must' was already passing off; in which case he would merely wander harmlessly about until the mahout came back and caught him. Moreover, I did not in the least want to shoot him. I decided that I would watch him for a little while to make sure that he did not turn savage again, and then go home.

But at that moment I glanced round at the crowd that had followed me. It was an immense crowd, two thousand at the least and growing every minute. It blocked the road for a long distance on either side. I looked at the sea of yellow faces above the garish clothes—faces all happy and excited over this bit of fun, all certain that the elephant was going to be shot. They were watching me as they would watch a conjurer about to perform a trick. They did not like me, but with the magical rifle in my hands I was momentarily worth watching. And suddenly I realized that I should have to shoot the elephant after all. The people expected it of me and I had got to do it; I could feel their two thousand wills pressing me forward, irresistibly. And it was at this moment, as I stood there with the rifle in my hands, that I first grasped the hollowness, the futility of the white man's dominion in the East. Here was I, the white man with his gun, standing in front of the unarmed native crowd—seemingly the leading actor of the piece; but in reality I was only an absurd puppet pushed to and fro by the will of those yellow faces behind. I perceived in this moment that when the white man turns tyrant it is his own freedom that he destroys. He becomes a sort of hollow, posing dummy, the conventionalized figure of a sahib. For it is the condition of his rule that he shall spend his life in trying to impress the 'natives' and so in every crisis he has got to do what the 'natives' expect of him. He wears a mask, and his face grows to fit it. I had got to shoot the elephant. I had committed myself to doing it when I sent for the rifle. A sahib has got to act like a sahib; he has got to appear resolute, to know his own mind and do definite things. To come all that way, rifle in hand, with two thousand people marching at my heels, and then to trail feebly away, having done nothing—no, that was impossible. The crowd would laugh at me. And my whole life, every white man's life in the East, was one long struggle not to be laughed at.

But I did not want to shoot the elephant. I watched him beating his bunch of grass against his knees, with that preoccupied grandmotherly air that elephants have. It seemed to me that it would be murder to shoot him. At that age I was not squeamish about killing animals, but I had never shot an elephant and never wanted to. (Somehow it always seems worse to kill a *large* animal.) Besides, there was the beast's owner to be considered. Alive, the elephant was worth at least a hundred pounds; dead, he would only be worth the value of his tusks, five pounds, possibly. But

I had got to act quickly. I turned to some experienced-looking Burmans who had been there when we arrived, and asked them how the elephant had been behaving. They all said the same thing: he took no notice of you if you left him alone, but he might charge if you went too close to him.

It was perfectly clear to me what I ought to do. I ought to walk up to within, say, twenty-five yards of the elephant and test his behaviour. If he charged, I could shoot; if he took no notice of me, it would be safe to leave him until the mahout came back. But also I knew that I was going to do no such thing. I was a poor shot with a rifle and the ground was soft mud into which one would sink at every step. If the elephant charged and I missed him, I should have about as much chance as a toad under a steamroller. But even then I was not thinking particularly of my own skin, only of the watchful yellow faces behind. For at that moment, with the crowd watching me, I was not afraid in the ordinary sense, as I would have been if I had been alone. A white man mustn't be frightened in front of 'natives'; and so, in general, he isn't frightened. The sole thought in my mind was that if anything went wrong those two thousand Burmans would see me pursued, caught, trampled on and reduced to a grinning corpse like that Indian up the hill. And if that happened it was quite probable that some of them would laugh. That would never do. There was only one alternative. I shoved the cartridges into the magazine and lay down on the road to get a better aim.

The crowd grew very still, and a deep, low, happy sigh, as of people who see the theatre curtain go up at last, breathed from innumerable throats. They were going to have their bit of fun after all. The rifle was a beautiful German thing with cross-hair sights. I did not then know that in shooting an elephant one would shoot to cut an imaginary bar running from ear-hole to ear-hole. I ought, therefore, as the elephant was sideways on, to have aimed straight at his ear-hole, actually I aimed several inches in front of this, thinking the brain would be further forward.

When I pulled the trigger I did not hear the bang or feel the kick—one never does when a shot goes home—but I heard the devilish roar of glee that went up from the crowd. In that instant, in too short a time, one would have thought, even for the bullet to get there, a mysterious, terrible change had come over the elephant. He neither stirred nor fell, but every line of his body had altered. He looked suddenly stricken, shrunken, immensely old, as though the frightful impact of the bullet had paralysed him without knocking him down. At last, after what seemed a long time—it might have been five seconds, I dare say—he sagged flabbily to his knees. His mouth slobbered. An enormous senility seemed to have settled upon him. One could have imagined him thousands of years old. I fired again into the same spot. At the second shot he did not collapse but climbed with desperate slowness to his feet and stood weakly upright, with legs sagging and head drooping. I fired a third time. That was the shot that did for him. You could see the agony of it jolt his whole body and knock the last remnant of strength from his legs. But in falling he seemed for a moment to rise, for as his hind legs collapsed beneath him he seemed to tower upward like a huge rock toppling, his trunk reaching skyward like a tree. He trumpeted, for the first and only time. And then down he came, his belly towards me, with a crash that seemed to shake the ground even where I lay.

I got up. The Burmans were already racing past me across the mud. It was obvious that the elephant would never rise again, but he was not dead. He was breathing very rhythmically with long rattling gasps, his great mound of a side painfully rising and falling. His mouth was wide open—I could see far down into caverns of pale pink throat. I waited a long time for him to die, but his breathing did not weaken. Finally I fired my two remaining shots into the spot where I thought his heart must be. The thick blood welled out of him like red velvet, but still he did not die. His body did not even jerk when the shots hit him, the tortured breathing continued without a pause. He was dying, very slowly and in great agony, but in some world remote from me where not even a bullet could damage him further. I felt that I had got to put an end to that dreadful noise. It seemed dreadful to see the great beast lying there, powerless to move and yet powerless to die, and not even to be able to finish him. I sent back for my small rifle and poured shot after shot into his heart and down his throat. They seemed to make no impression. The tortured gasps continued as steadily as the ticking of a clock.

In the end I could not stand it any longer and went away. I heard later that it took him half an hour to die. Burmans were bringing das and baskets even before I left, and I was told they had stripped his body almost to the bones by the afternoon.

Afterwards, of course, there were endless discussions about the shooting of the elephant. The owner was furious, but he was only an Indian and could do nothing. Besides, legally I had done the right thing, for a mad elephant has to be killed, like a mad dog, if its owner fails to control it. Among the Europeans opinion was divided. The older men said I was right, the younger men said it was a damn shame to shoot an elephant for killing a coolie, because an elephant was worth more than any damn Coringhee coolie. And afterwards I was very glad that the coolie had been killed; it put me legally in the right and it gave me a sufficient pretext for shooting the elephant. I often wondered whether any of the others grasped that I had done it solely to avoid looking a fool.

NINE

~

DEATH OF A PATRIARCH*

DAVID DAVIDAR

The pain had been unexpected, so intense that it had driven every other sensation from his body. Daniel didn't know if he was breathing, if he had screamed out in agony; all he could think of was that what he was experiencing was more than he could tolerate. And then, with the swiftness with which it had clutched him, it was gone, leaving behind only a feeling of great discomfort. He couldn't speak, he could barely breathe, a mist obscured his sight, but he wasn't afraid...

The news of Daniel's decline spread rapidly through the colony. In less than an hour, the house was packed. The doctor would evict people from the sick-room, but they'd filter back. He lost his temper on one occasion and shouted, 'Get out, get out all of you. This man is fighting for his life, he needs air, he needs peace and

*This extract is taken from *The House of Blue Mangoes* by David Davidar, published by Aleph Book Company, 2013.

quiet.' He turned to Ramdoss and said, 'Can't you get them to leave the room, and stay out of it! This man is too sick to be moved, otherwise I would have him taken to hospital immediately.'

The room was cleared at once, but nobody went far. The hot, airless corridors and passages of the mansion were clogged with people waiting with a variety of expressions, boredom, grief or the blank, unseeing look of people who have mastered the art of patiently waiting for nothing in particular. All through the morning more and more people trekked to the House of Blue Mangoes, drawn by a shared sense of grief at the imminent passing of the man who had been the dominant presence in their world as far back as they could remember. In the room where Daniel lay, there were still too many people, but Ramdoss and the doctor had at least managed to restrict it to close family and the priest. Two large nephews blocked the door, and politely but firmly refused everyone else entry.

The fog still filled Daniel's head, but his discomfort had lessened. He tried to use the breathing techniques enjoined by the siddha masters. Gradually his suffering eased. He sensed people around him, but couldn't make out individual faces. Nothing but blurry images in his vision, although in his mind's eye there was now some clarity—he saw Lily where he would have expected to see her, by his bed, her eyes shut in prayer; Ramu, tears running down his cheeks; Solomon and Charity; his sisters Rachel and Miriam, who had fought with him so vigorously; Aaron, such a beautiful youth; Thirumoolar, Dr Pillai, Father Ashworth. But why was everyone so sorrowful? He was at peace now, the pain was bearable; this passage was something he was prepared to negotiate, it was something he wished for.

He felt a pricking sensation on his skin, and then a voice that he couldn't understand came faintly to him. He tried to open his eyes but they didn't seem to be obeying his will. Better to concentrate on his breathing; if he could regulate that, everything else would fall into place.

The silence of the room was broken by a loud voice. Miriam, who appeared to have fallen into a trance, was shouting, sweat drenching her face and blouse, her eyes intense and bright, 'Anna, anna, can you see him now? Can you see our Saviour the Lord who is waiting for you?'

Galvanized into activity by the commotion, the people in the room surged forward. 'Clear the room. At once,' the doctor and Ramdoss were shouting, pushing people away from Daniel's bed. His grandson Daniel dropped to the floor and scrambled through the legs of the adults, an empty test tube in his hand; this he thrust under the dying man's nostrils and held for a long moment. Trace elements inside reacted to Daniel's breath and the inside of the test tube clouded over. The boy stoppered it swiftly and returned the way he had come. Miriam kept screaming, 'Anna, can you see the Lord?' Ramdoss continued to shove people out of the room, the priest murmured prayers and Lily stood by the bedside as if carved from stone.

A rumour snaked its way outside that Dr Daniel Dorai was dead, and immediately a high-pitched keening began, rising and falling in the thick, humid air, setting the birds clumsily stirring in the branches of the large mango tree in front of the house.

Dr Dorai was oblivious to all this. He was walking down the beach in bright sunshine with Father Ashworth, looking not at the brittle surf, but at the sand at his feet where the shells left behind by the rushing water gleamed like polished stone. To his astonishment, the shells seemed to be moving of their own accord. Excitedly, he pointed this out to the priest. Father Ashworth picked up a shell and showed him the long, fleshy feet of the mollusc, its imperceptible grip on his finger, its tenacious hold on life, amidst the thunder of the sea. A great light filled his head, an instant after the pain swamped him with an intensity he knew signalled the end…then he was abruptly free of it.

All we can hope for, when the time comes, Ramdoss thought, as he watched the doctors try in vain to revive the man who was the centre of his universe, is that we die well, having overcome our terror of never again walking with friends, eating fruit off the trees, anticipating surprises... That wasn't the only fear to be mastered, he realized the next instant—when we prepare to die, not only do we have to be accepting of what we leave behind, we also have to be prepared for what awaits us: a good place or a bad place, rebirth or union with the Divine.

~

Some weeks after Daniel died, Ramdoss found a copy of the Upanishads in his room, with some passages neatly underlined in blue ink. One of these was verse 13 of chapter 3 of the second Brahmana of the *Brhad-aranyaka Upanishad*, which maintained that when a person dies:

The speech enters into fire
The breath into air
The eye into the sun
The mind into the moon
The sense of hearing into the quarters
The self into the ether
The hair on the body into herbs
The hair on the head into trees
And the blood and the semen into water.

Another passage Daniel had underlined was the reply of Yajnavalkya, the Divine Teacher, to the question of what became of the self, the life force, when a person passed away:

As a goldsmith, taking a piece of gold
Turns it into another, newer and more beautiful shape,
Even so does this self after having thrown away its body
And dispelled its ignorance,
Make itself into another, newer and more beautiful shape
Like that of the fathers, or the gandharvas, or of the Gods
Or of Prajapati, or of Brahma, or of other beings...

Two further passages were so heavily underlined that the ink had soaked through to the other side of the paper. They compared a dying man to a king who was about to depart. Policemen, judges, soldiers, attendants, village leaders, other dignitaries cluster around the departing potentate. Just so do the senses gather around the self when a person is on the point of dying. The powers of the senses wane and descend into the heart…the point of the heart lights up and by that light the self departs, either through the eyes or through the head or through the other apertures of the body. With the self go the senses, taking flight to another world. As his senses failed one by one, perhaps Dr Dorai thought of the image, as his living self fled up to the sun.

Chinni was a seven-year-old from a village in which the shacks had been built on the left side of the road. She sat still and aimlessly watched the road. What she wore barely resembled a skirt and a blouse. Dirty, darned over and over again, her clothes were falling to shreds now because there was no cloth left to hold the stitches. She was pretty. The snot below her nose could, no doubt, be cleaned. The dirt on her body could, no doubt, be washed off. What of her hair—it could be brushed and neatly oiled. What of her clothes—one could get new clothes and she could wear them. If she had flowers in her hair, she would herself look like a flower. Even without any of these, Chinni was a pretty girl; she had pleasant features and sparkling eyes!

Now and then a car or a lorry passed by. The farmhands emerged from the village chatting noisily, swinging their staffs. Occasionally, a fierce wind blew. A boy appeared on the road that Chinni was staring at; he came from the side of the village where the cement houses were, across the road from the shacks. He was eating a banana. In his left hand, he held another banana. He was clearly enjoying the banana he was eating, biting it, licking it, nibbling it, bit by bit. Chinni watched him, drooling. Her eyes sparkled with hope. She watched him intently for a couple of seconds. She came to her feet. Dragging her feet, she walked slowly across the road to the boy. He slowed down but did not stop. He continued to eat. Now it was hard to tell whether he was really eating the banana or merely licking it and pretending to eat it for it did not seem to be diminishing in size.

Chinni looked into the boy's face. He returned the glance. She kept staring. He did not turn away. She watched the fruit in his mouth, the fruit in his hand, her glance shifting from his mouth to hand, hand to mouth, looking straight into his eyes, begging him wordlessly. He turned away as if he had not got the message.

'Can't you give me some?' Chinni asked, but the boy paid no attention.

'Give me a little!'

'Why?' he drawled.

'A little?' she pleaded.

'No, don't I want it? I won't give you any,' he said.

'A little, a small bit?'

'No.'

'Just a little.'

'I won't, I said.'

'Just as much as an ant's head.'

'No!'

Chinni's mouth watered, her eyes welled up. Her heart turned to water. A wave of misery swelled within her. She collected her spirits, stretched out her arm and tried to snatch the banana from him like an eagle. Like the mother hen that protects its chicks, he shielded the banana from her and dashed into the village located on the right side of the road. Chasing him, Chinni stumbled and fell on the cement road. She grazed her elbow, and her forehead was streaked with dirt. Chinni got up with tear-filled eyes. She glanced at the boy. He showed her the banana as if to offer it to her, but then stuck out his tongue, and, making a face, walked into the village.

Chinni stopped crying, wiped her nose, eyes, forehead, and elbow with the edge of her skirt, and flopped down under a tamarind tree, trying hard not to cry. It has been three days since she or her mother, sister, and little brother had eaten anything. They were all starving. Chinni, her sister and brother had drained the water in the pot by daybreak. Her mother did not stir out of her bed; she was heavily pregnant, about to give birth and extremely weak. If her father got the day's wages they ate, otherwise they filled their bellies with water. If he returned home, they at least had water to drink, otherwise it was complete starvation. Her father had not come home for three days.

Her elder sister at least carried some water home like their father. Her mother would send her sister to the neighbour's to borrow a measure of rice. But they had nothing either. Everybody who lived on the village on the left side of the road had to scrape a living and nobody had anything to spare. On learning this, Chinni was seized by a fit of anger. She had taken to going to houses where she could smell rice cooking, or see smoke rising from the hearth. She would circle these houses, peep in and say to herself, 'They ate rice, washed the vessels, and turned the rice pot upside down to dry.' She had done this for the last three days, weeping silently.

That night her belly smouldered sleeplessly like a haystack on which an ember had fallen accidentally. Chinni felt death would be a relief to the suffering of an empty stomach in the monsoon. Earlier, whenever Chinni felt hungry during the night, she had been content to wait for the day in the hope that it would bring food. But for three successive dawns, she had awoken hungry. When day was about to break again, Chinni felt more miserable than happy. She could not bear to give hunger its irrevocable victory.

When she had lain curled up in hunger last night, it had rained on the hut like a curse on a poor man. She shivered in the cold on the wet mat she lay on, as hunger gnawed her until dawn. She woke up early in the morning and felt miserable. Her emaciated belly was visible to everyone in the village.

∽

Now, pulling her arms and legs up against her empty belly, with her cold body and wet clothes, she sat under the tamarind tree with an aching heart. The sun had not yet risen. Perhaps it was afraid that if it rose it might have to give witness to the vagaries of fate. A huge cloud rested on the hill that loomed behind the village, it seemed hesitant to release more rain, as though afraid of being shrunk, melted, or annihilated.

'Chinni!' A harsh voice called out.

Chinni looked up. In front of her was the brother of the

boy who had kept on eating the banana. Chinni was frightened.

'Can't you reply?' he asked, glaring at her.

She muttered, 'What do you want?'

'Did you snatch the banana from him?'

'No.'

'Tell the truth!'

'No.'

'If you lie, I'll pinch your cheeks.'

'No'

'Chchir!' he snarled at her. 'How dare you harass him? You dirty little bitch.' Furiously, he continued to abuse her. Chinni was about to break into tears.

'Beggar. Scoundrel.'

'You are one!'

'How dare you? What do you mean by that? Say it again, I'll slap you hard.'

'You are one!' she uttered the words again.

He kept his word as if he would otherwise lose his claim to the lineage of the legendary Harishchandra, known for speaking the truth. He slapped her hard on the cheek. A little girl, her little belly fastened against her backbone after suffering gnawing hunger for days. Chinni fell to the ground and even the earth hurt her. If she cried out 'Amma', her mother would not hear. Even if she had heard, she would not have come to her rescue. Even if she were to come, she would not have said anything to him. There was no question of hitting him back. If she were to hit him, she would suffer greater humiliation. Her father was not home, so he would not come. The boy's brother had no trouble and went away safely.

Chinni felt an ache in her belly as if her guts had knotted up. She could not even muster enough energy to get up from where she had fallen. The boy had done her a service by slapping her hard enough to make her forget the hunger, which had gripped her like a demon and had been haunting her like a ghost for the last three days. The blow filled her belly, abating her hunger.

The breeze whipped about lightly. There was a drizzle, a shower. But the cloud on the hill had not moved, it lay there like a shopkeeper sitting tight in front of his cash box. There were no raindrops under the tamarind tree. The night before, rain had washed the road clean and it was not yet dirty. Raindrops fell now and then like water dripping from just-washed hair. The bell from the higher elementary school beside the village rang urgently. Affected by hunger, cold, and the blows she had received, Chinni looked up bewildered at a father taking his toddler son to school and hung her head.

∽

Her father was not home. Until the other day, they had starved because he had no work when it rained. When her father had left home, the stove was damp and had not been lit since. For a twenty-five-kilometre stretch, flooding streams and rivulets had breached the road at several places. To clear the way for traffic, it had to be repaired at once. The supervisor had come searching for labourers, and her father had gone along with him three days ago. He had not returned since.

Chinni did not know whether the road was repaired or when her father would return home. She got up. Her legs were wobbly, she swayed like a madman, a drunk, one possessed. A gust of wind slashed her back. Hunger scorched her guts. The thought of the bruise on her elbow, the slap on her cheek, and the mud on her forehead drove her to a frenzy. More than the injuries themselves, the manner in which they had been inflicted on her brought tears to her eyes.

Just as swollen eyes are emptied of all tears after persistent sobbing, so it had stopped raining, as if the skies had no more energy to shower or drizzle. A lorry carrying boulders from the quarry was approaching, rattling as it came. Chinni looked at the lorry, at first uninterestedly, then with curiosity, and later with hope. When the lorry drew close, shuddering loudly, she stepped forward. The lorry was inching forward steadily with a full load, like a woman heavy with child. When the lorry was level with her, Chinni ran out in front of it as if possessed. The driver saw her and cried, 'Hey!' The owner saw her and cried out, 'Rai!' Shrieks and shouts. The lorry stopped with a screeching of brakes. The lorry was there. Chinni was there in front of the lorry. Within an inch of it! Chinni hung her head and just stood there, biting her nails as if she were innocent. When she saw two pairs of eyes from the lorry fixed on her, she writhed, hunger deepening within her.

'Who are you, miserable stray? Do you want to die?' shouted the driver.

'You wretch! You want to die and kill us too?' the owner cried.

'Out, out,' the driver yelled, pushing her.

'Out, out,' added the owner, shoving her.

And so Chinni was back under the tamarind tree. An old tamarind tree, a tree that seemed to have stood there forever. The back of her head rested on the trunk. The tree shed drops of water like a mother weeping at her daughter's suffering.

The road looked washed and wiped clean, the water drying up. Wild shrubs on the roadside had caught leaves, bits of papers and other waste. They looked muddy with layers of dirt. On the side of the road, rainwater had carved runnels into the sandy soil, undulating like an emaciated man's ribs.

By the time her sister and brother showed up, there were no tears in Chinni's eyes. Her eyes had dried up like the water in wells during summer. 'Why are you looking so dirty?' her sister asked curiously, looking at her muddy body. Chinni was silent. 'Can't you talk? Did you not hear me?' Chinni did not reply. Her sister looked into her face intently. Chinni lowered her head. Her brother grabbed her shoulder and shook her.

The clothes of her brother and sister were worn and patched, their hair was unoiled like straw. Water dripped from their heads and cheeks. The little fellow was shivering with cold. 'Amma is groaning. She has been calling out, "Chinni, Chinni!" Come, let us go home,' he said.

When she heard the word Amma, Chinni began shaking. She wanted to cry, thinking of Amma near delivery, unable to stir out of bed. She had no food, nor did Amma. She could move about, but her mother could not. She was better off. Chinni could not bear to see her mother's pain. If she did, she would not be able to control herself from breaking down. No energy to cry, her heart ached, though she remained dry-eyed. Water trickled from her sodden hair, down her cheeks and disappeared. Drops from her head disappeared into her lips. Pushing up her hair with both hands, she glanced at her brother and sister by turn.

Her sister was ten. She helped Amma with household chores. When Amma fell ill, her sister had taken over all her work. She bathed her younger brother and Chinni, wiped them dry and dressed them in fresh clothes, if there were any. She loved Chinni and her little brother and shared with them whatever she could buy to eat. After giving them both what she had, she would sometimes go around the whole day chewing on her empty mouth. If a handful of rice was left at the bottom of the pot, she would quietly give it to Chinni and her brother.

On the night their father left home with the construction gang, Amma had given all the rice that was left in their shack to the elder sister without keeping anything for herself. She in turn gave it all to Chinni and her brother. Chinni, too, did not feel like eating. She felt sorry for her brother. He had greedily gobbled down the few mouthfuls given to him. It was over even before his little belly filled. He drank water and cuddling up to Amma, fell asleep in her bed. Chinni and her sister also went to bed but could not sleep because their father was away. Her mother told her elder sister, 'See! The little one has also grown to be like you. Have you seen her giving food to her little brother without eating any herself? It doesn't really matter whether we have anything to eat or drink, your affection for each other is more than enough.'

When she heard these words, Chinni was happy, but can hunger help one to be happy? Her sister and mother fell asleep but Chinni could not sleep. Spotting the eyes of a cat in the dark, Chinni shut her eyes tightly and did not open them until daybreak. Before she dropped off to sleep, Chinni thought about her little brother. He was a silly little fellow. He could not play a single game. He could not even hop properly. He drooled and barely spoke twenty words a day. He was barely three! He would not stir out of the house unless accompanied by both his sisters. His tottering gait was cute, his lisping and stuttering words, too, were quite endearing.

~

Almost a year ago, children playing on the same road were running from tree to tree. Some adults scolded them but that did not stop them from playing. They all cheered Chinni, saying that only she could run across to the other side of the road, touch the tree and come back before the lorry got there—only she had the guts to do this. As usual, Chinni dashed across the road, touched the tree and turned back, running as fast as she could. She did not see how close the lorry was. The children were shrieking. She could not make out whether this was out of delight that she had returned before the lorry, or whether it was a warning that the lorry was closing in on her. She heard a loud shriek. That was the last thing she heard. When she opened her eyes, everything had gone quiet. When she saw her mother and father, Chinni felt like crying. When she heard that she was out of danger but had lost a lot of blood, Chinni felt happy, not knowing why.

The lorry owner had waited until Chinni came around. When she regained consciousness, a great weight had lifted from him, as if he had offloaded a full lorry. Much relieved, he had driven away. From that day onwards, the lorry owner had paid Chinni's family a hundred rupees a month for four months, and given her food as compensation for six months. Those days Chinni enjoyed heavenly delights, lying on her simple jute cot. When she woke up, someone or the other served her food and looked after her. They ate only after she had eaten.

A hundred rupees a month for her sake! More than what her father and mother earned. This money was a symbol of the union of darkness and light when the lamp of her life breath had flickered terribly. This money was a wildflower that had sprouted on a grave. This money was the price, the measure of the earth that mingled with human blood. This money was the flag that showed the nobility of a rich man and the servility of a poor man.

Her parents who would have loved the child even without this money, loved her all the more because of the money. This money brought them happiness. Chinni felt proud that she had earned the money, and that she had repaid her parents' debt.

In Chinni's view, food meant pouring rasam on a fistful of rice. It was the most desirable food until then. She had never known that there could be any other kind of food. She did not know that bread and eggs could be her daily fare, nor did she know that delicacies such as bread and butter or bread and jam existed. When she tasted the food the lorry owner brought from town, she realized how ignorant she had been. When she ate bread and eggs, her tongue had felt like a garden blossoming with luxuriant, colourful flowers. When she ate bread and butter, she felt as if she were gliding effortlessly over slush, her body had felt like cotton wool. When the bread and jam slipped down her throat, it was sweet and sour, soft and hard.

When she removed the skin and ate grapes, they had disappeared down her throat, belly, and inner parts like a stone thrown into a well sinks slowly out of the sunlight. When an orange, a sweet lime, or a country orange was peeled, its seeds removed and the pulp put in her mouth, the juice overflowed, swelling like a spring, spreading a pleasant taste all over her throat. An apple eaten in the same way tasted like cream. There was no need to chew, no need to bite, no work for her teeth. It melted in the warmth of her tongue and slid down her throat. When she ate bananas of different varieties, centuries of hunger seemed to just disappear.

A piece of jalebi made her mouth water sweetly. When she chewed on a Mysore pak, each tooth came alive as if it had witnessed a great revelation. When she ate a laddu, it tasted like ambrosia from the crumbling foundations of heaven itself. When she put a scoopful of spicy boondi into her mouth, satisfaction spread along every nerve.

Varieties of biscuits: sweet, salty, pungent, and hot—Chinni soon gathered that man had scooped out all the tastes God had created and filled biscuits with them. The others in the house ate whatever was left after Chinni ate. It was a stroke of good fortune that in Chinni's house they were able to eat such good food for six long months.

Every day Chinni stood on the road waiting for the lorry, leaping up in joy whenever it came. When she took home the food given by the owner or the driver, she saw fortune in the lorry, god in the owner, and joy in her mother and father. All this made her extremely happy.

After six months, when the gash on her forehead disappeared, no more fruits came her way even when the lorry did. Even if the owner smiled, he did not give her sweets. Every time he stopped the lorry and enquired, 'Are you well?' and drove off, she was miserable and cried. Gradually, the lorry ceased to stop.

Her stomach revolted when she had to go back to eating red chilli pickle with her taste buds that had grown used to bread, when she had to drink rasam or other sour things with the throat that had swallowed fruit juices, when she had to eat ordinary sambar and rice with the tongue that had tasted sweets. Hunger was a gift given by God. Gradually, hunger cured the nauseous feelings that regular food evoked in her. She got used to her daily fare, although at times she craved the luxuries she had eaten for a while.

Chinni had waited for the lorry to stop for the last six months and was disappointed. Why had the lorry owner fed her so well for such a long time? Why had he suddenly stopped doing so? She thought hard and tried to find the answers to these questions but came up with nothing.

What could she do to get the rich food again? For six months, this question had churned over and over again in her little brain.

What could she do?

ᔑ

On the night that she had lain hungry for three days, when she had been tempted by the boy with the banana, and had been slapped by his brother, the answer to the question that had been obsessing her flashed through her mind. Hunger burned her insides, the cold tightened its grip on her skin. When the house shook under the lash of the rains, her Amma groaned. Her father was away but all these were swamped by the excitement her insight generated. She was unable to sleep that night. She was more anxious than the sun for daybreak. She got up as the darkness faded, went to the road, looked up and down, and went back home at least ten times. At last she reached the tamarind tree and sat under it from nine o'clock onwards.

The sun still seemed to be snoring under a tightly wrapped blanket. Hiding and flitting out from behind the hilltop, a big cloud came into view like a recruiting officer with small clouds trailing it. The wind blew fiercely and pushed the clouds forward. Suddenly it began to rain, the raindrops falling like well-aimed bullets.

Chinni did not stir from where she sat. She did not move even when the slanting rain slammed into her body. The children playing on the road ran home. In the village on the right of the road, where the concrete houses were, except for the roar of the rain, not a mouse stirred. In the village on the left, the rain seemed vengeful. On both sides of the road, the village was deserted. Not a soul to be seen. Rain everywhere. On the hill, on the fields, on the houses, on the trees, on the road, rain all over. It rained like the universal truth. As the sky poured down rain, the earth threw up a great chill. The cold and the rain were Chinni's only companions.

The leaves had become heavy, the branches heavier and the trees hung their heads, drooping like a poor man in despair. A nearby haystack soaked with water shrank until it looked like a starved belly. Chinni watched the road intently. When she saw the lorry coming like the sun breaking through the clouds in the morning, joy exploded in her. The same lorry that had become familiar all the year around. As the lorry drew level with her, every drop of blood in her body broke and leapt out.

The lorry, like the owner's goodness, was approaching. It looked like mother's love, like God's kindness coming face to face with her. It approached like bread, fruit, laddus, and biscuits, like food filling an empty belly. Chinni came to her feet. The lorry was closing in on her, moment by moment. Her hope grew; her blood surged within her, as if her hunger was being satisfied. The loaded lorry moved forward heavily. The rain slanted. A blanket of dimness from the sky to the earth. Daytime, but the village was silent. Not a soul stirred.

The lorry was almost upon her. Chinni ran across the road. Until then the driver had not seen Chinni. Then he saw her, a smiling Chinni. When he recognized Chinni's face, he became glum. The cheroot that the owner was smoking slipped from his stiff fingers when he saw Chinni, a smiling Chinni running in front of the lorry.

Chinni kept smiling. There was no happiness in that smile, only despair, hunger, pain...no life in the smile, no radiance. That smile was not a smile. In that smile was sorrow, misery, despair, prayer, request and a plea!

In the past it had been the driver's habit to smile back at Chinni. This time he did not. It was a ritual for the owner to respond to her smile with an answering smile. He did not do so either. The driver's hands shook, his legs shook. The fully-laden lorry surged forward. It was raining, the road was slippery. The driver pressed down on the brake pedal. The lorry did not stop. The brakes did not respond.

Chinni was in front of their eyes. Pretty Chinni, smart Chinni, Chinni who had narrowly escaped death, Chinni whom the driver was very fond of. The owner's heart trembled. His nerves stretched until it seemed they would break. It seemed to the driver that his limbs were no longer obeying him, his hands turned the steering wheel of their own volition. The lorry swerved but did not stop.

Chinni saw the lorry swerving. But she could not bear to think of the ambrosia-like lorry, that lorry that provided food, escaping from her. She turned in the same direction the lorry turned. She moved where it moved. She stood in front of it, obstructing it.

'Chinni!' howled the driver. He turned the steering wheel again. The lorry swung on to the road again. He stepped on the brake pedal forcefully. With a screech, like the groaning of an old man, the lorry stopped. Chinni was not in sight. Now she fell in the middle of the road. The last time she had fallen by the side of the lorry. This time she fell in front of it. The lorry had not been able to stop in time. Chinni thought she was losing consciousness, and she did.

Something hit her belly. Was it the hand of her mother or her father? Would she see them when she came to? Would Amma caress her hungry belly? Chinni no longer felt anything. The lorry was there. The road was there. Chinni was on it. At last its brakes worked and the lorry stopped. It moved while stopping. Stopped while moving. One of the front wheels felt something like a stone obstructing it; it climbed over it, and down the other side. The minute the lorry stopped, the driver and the owner leapt out on either side.

Chinni was nowhere to be seen. From under the lorry, blood mingled with rainwater and flowed red into a roadside ditch.

∽

In the middle of the road, its belly ripped open, blood splattered everywhere, its legs fastened to the road, flattened like a dosai, a bullfrog. A big, bellowing frog. One that had cried, leapt, jumped, thought, wept, laughed and one that had been troubled by hunger. And one, which, with its stomach severed, was hungry no more.

ACKNOWLEDGEMENTS

Grateful acknowledgement is made to these copyright holders for permission to reprint copyrighted material in this volume:

'The Ghosts of Mrs Gandhi' by Amitav Ghosh. Copyright © Amitav Ghosh, 2002, used by permission of The Wylie Agency (UK) Limited.

'The Funeral' by Ruskin Bond, copyright © Ruskin Bond, reprinted by permission of the author.

'Pyre' by Amitava Kumar, published in *Granta* 130, 2015, copyright © Amitava Kumar, 2015, reprinted by permission of the author.

'Seed' by Mahasweta Devi, translated by Ipshita Chanda, original © Tathagata Bhattacharya, 2016, English translation © Seagull Books, 2002, published by arrangement with Seagull Books and the translator.

'Being Mortal' by Atul Gawande, excerpted from *Being Mortal* by Atul Gawande. Copyright © Atul Gawande, 2014, reprinted by permission of the author.

'The Shroud' by Munshi Premchand, extracted from *The Greatest Urdu Stories Ever Told*, selected and translated by Muhammad Umar Memon, published by Aleph Book Company, 2017, English language copyright © The Estate of Muhammad Umar Memon, reprinted by permission of Nakako Memon.

'The Portrait of a Lady' by Khushwant Singh, first published in *The Collected Stories of Khushwant Singh*, Ravi Dayal Publisher, 1989, reprinted by permission of Mala Dayal.

'Death of a Patriarch', extracted from *The House of Blue Mangoes* by David Davidar, published by Aleph Book Company, 2013. Copyright © David Davidar, 2002, 2013.

NOTES ON THE CONTRIBUTORS

Ruskin Bond (born 1934) is the author of several bestselling novels and collections of short stories, essays, and poems. These include *The Room on the Roof* (winner of the John Llewellyn Rhys Prize), *A Flight of Pigeons*, *The Night Train at Deoli*, *Time Stops at Shamli*, *Our Trees Still Grow in Dehra* (winner of the Sahitya Akademi Award), *Angry River*, *The Blue Umbrella*, *Delhi is Not Far*, *Rain in the Mountains*, *Tigers for Dinner*, *Tales of Fosterganj*, *A Gathering of Friends*, *Upon An Old Wall Dreaming*, *Small Towns, Big Stories, Unhurried Tales*, A *Gallery of Rascals, Rhododendrons in the Mist*, and *Miracle at Happy Bazaar: My Very Best Stories for Children*.

Ipshita Chanda (born 1961) teaches in the Department of Comparative Literature at the English and Foreign Languages University, Hyderabad. She has authored *Packaging Freedom: Feminism and Popular Culture* and *Selfing the City: Women Migrants and Their Lives in Calcutta*, and co-edited *Shaping the Discourse* (with Jayeeta Bagchi) and *Locating Cultural Change* (with Partha Pratim Basu). Her translations include *Bitter Soil*, a translation of Mahasweta Devi's selected stories.

David Davidar (born 1958) is the author of three novels, *The House of Blue Mangoes* (2002), which was published in sixteen countries and was a *New York Times* Notable Book; *The Solitude of Emperors* (2007), which was shortlisted for a Commonwealth Writers' Prize; and *Ithaca* (2011). He is also the editor of *A Clutch of Indian Masterpieces*. Davidar is the co-founder of Aleph Book Company.

Mahasweta Devi (1926–2016) was a noted social activist and Bengali writer. Her first book, *The Queen of Jhansi*, was published in 1956. She published twenty collections of short stories and close to a hundred novels. She won several literary prizes including the Sahitya Akademi Award in 1979 for her novel *Aranyer Adhikar*.

Kolakaluri Enoch (born 1939) is a distinguished scholar, critic, and Telugu writer. His collection of short stories *Oorabaavi* is considered the first volume of Telugu Dalit short stories. He taught Telugu literature for decades in SKD University and is a former vice-chancellor of Sri Venkateswara University, Tirupati. He has won the Padma Sri and the 29th Moortidevi Award of Bharatiya Jnanpith in 2015, and has received multiple honours from the Andhra Pradesh Sahitya Akademi. A unique mark of his writing is that Dalit and socio-economic issues remain in the background against which human dramas of compassion and cruelty take place.

Atul Gawande (born 1965) is CEO of Haven, the Amazon, Berkshire Hathaway, JP Morgan Chase healthcare venture, and a globally recognized surgeon, writer, and public health leader. For more than twenty years, he has been a surgeon at Brigham and Women's Hospital and a professor at Harvard T. H. Chan School of Public Health and Harvard Medical School. He is the founder and chairman of Ariadne Labs, a joint center for health systems innovation, and chairman of Lifebox, a nonprofit organization making surgery safer globally. Gawande has also been a staff writer for the *New Yorker* since 1998 and written four *New York Times* bestselling books: *Complications*, *Better*, *The Checklist Manifesto,* and *Being Mortal*: *Medicine and What Matters in the End*. He is the winner of two National Magazine Awards, AcademyHealth's Impact Award for highest research impact on healthcare, a MacArthur Fellowship, and the Lewis Thomas Award for writing about science.

Amitav Ghosh (born 1956) is the author of eleven highly acclaimed works of fiction and non-fiction which include the Booker Prize shortlisted *Sea of Poppies* (Book One of the Ibis Trilogy), *River of Smoke*, *The Glass Palace*, *The Shadow Lines* and, most recently, *Gun Island*. He has won numerous prizes, some of which are the Jnanpith Award, Sahitya Akademi Award, the Pushcart Prize and the Grinzane Cavour Prize. He divides his time between New York and India.

C. L .L. Jayaprada (born 1954) retired from Andhra University as professor of English after teaching various literatures of the world in English and Translation Studies for three decades. A bilingual translator, she published several Nobel speeches and Australian stories in Telugu translation as she did Telugu stories in English in *Indian Literature*, *Sarasa*, *Chandrabhaga*, *JSL*, *Journal of Literature & Aesthetics*, *South Asian Review*, and *Routes*, a British Council book. The story in *Routes* titled 'Foxtrot' on Anglo Indians in India won her the Jyesta Translation Award. Her published books of translation include *He Conquered the Jungle*, *Stories of Tenali Raman*, and *Purusha Ahamkaraniki Sawal*.

Amitava Kumar (born 1963) is the author of several books, including *Writing Badly is Easy*, *A Matter of Rats: A Short Biography of Patna* and *The Lovers: A Novel*, published by Aleph. His first novel, *Home Products* (2007), was shortlisted for the Crossword Prize, and his non-fiction report, *A Foreigner Carrying in the Crook of His Arm a Tiny Bomb* (2010) was given the Page Turner Award. Kumar's writing has appeared in the *New Yorker*, *The Guardian*, *New York Times*, *Caravan*, *Harper's*, and *Vanity Fair*. His essay 'Pyre', first published in *Granta*, was selected by Jonathan Franzen for *Best*

American Essays, 2016. He was awarded a Guggenheim Fellowship in 2016. Kumar is Professor of English at Vassar College.

Muhammad Umar Memon (1939–2018) was a critic, short story writer, and translator of numerous works of Urdu fiction, most recently the bestselling *The Greatest Urdu Stories Ever Told*. He was editor of the *Annual of Urdu Studies* (1993–2014).

George Orwell (1903–50) was the pseudonym of Eric Arthur Blair, born in Motihari (Bihar) in British India. He was a prominent English novelist, essayist, journalist, and critic, famous for his dystopian novels on totalitarian regimes, *Animal Farm* (1945) and *Nineteen Eighty-Four* (1949).

Munshi Premchand (1880–1936) was one of the earliest writers of Urdu fiction. His phenomenal output was marked by his passionate belief in the transformative agency of literature in ridding society of its myriad social and religious ills. He first wrote in Urdu, but later switched to Hindi in view of the poor market for Urdu books. He was the author of more than a dozen novels, over two hundred short stories, several essays and translations of foreign literary works. Some of his novels and countless stories have been translated into English and other languages. His last novel, *Godaan* (The Offering of a Cow), finished just before his death in 1936, and the story 'Kafan' (The Shroud) rank among his most engaging and enduring works.